Whipstock

Whipstock

Barb Howard

NEWEST PRESS

National Library of Canada Cataloguing in Publication Data
Howard, Barb, 1962-
Whipstock

(Nunatak fiction)
ISBN 1-896300-56-1

I. Title. II. Series.
PS8565.O828W44 2001   C813'.6   C2001-910789-7
PR9199.4.H68W44 2001

Editor for the Press: Anne Nothof
Cover and interior design: Ruth Linka
Cover image: Marilyn Ledingham
Author photo: Gold Photography

Some of these chapters, in slightly different form, have been previously published in *Dandelion* and *Room of One's Own*.

Canadian   Patrimoine
Heritage   canadien

NeWest Press acknowledges the support of the Canada Council for the Arts and the Alberta Foundation for the Arts for our publishing program. We also acknowledge the financial support of the Government of Canada through the Book Publishing Industry Development Program (BPIDP) for our publishing activities.

NeWest Press
201–8540–109 Street
Edmonton, Alberta T6G 1E6
(780) 432-9427
www.newestpress.com

01 02 03 04 05   5 4 3 2 1

PRINTED AND BOUND IN CANADA

To my Mom
Margaret Elizabeth Howard
who will always be an inspiration

Acknowledgements

Barrels of thanks to:

Mike, Ross and Stuart Gardner for love, ideas, support and distractions;

Aritha van Herk for experience, understanding, and challenging classrooms;

Joan and Frank Gardner, Margo Hamilton, and Angela Bose for warm, creative childcare that always exceeds a fussy mother's standards;

Mary Howard for feedback, encouragement and sisterly celebrations;

Anne Nothof for final edits and late night phone calls;

John Howard for engineering and brotherly support; and

all those oil patchers, especially Lorraine Grant, who took the time to read and fact find and advise.

Also, the nod of a pump jack to the following sources of inspiration and research:

Garstad-Rosenau, Elsie. (comp. and ed.) Oil Patch Recollections of "The Way Things Were." Edmonton: Lifelines, 1977.

Gould, Ed. *Oil*. British Columbia: Hancock, 1976.

Kerr, Aubrey. *Atlantic no. 3*. Calgary: Kerr, 1986.

Kerr, Aubrey. *Corridors of Time*. Calgary: Kerr, 1988.

Lougheed, Tim. "fill 'er up with bio diesel." *Calgary Herald*. 2 Jul 1999. WS1.

Silverman, Eliane. *Last Best West*. Calgary, Fifth House, 1998.

Steinberg, Theodore. *Slide Mountain*. Los Angeles: U of California P, 1995.

I

"Weevil Sandwich," Nellie writes on the sign at the entrance to the cafeteria. She caps her pen and steps back into Sauerkraut.

"That's taking quite a liberty with the Western Sandwich," Sauerkraut says, crossing her arms.

"I think of it more as giving a liberty." Nellie uses the pen to make a flourish in the air, then pops the pen into her apron pocket. "The employees like it."

Sauerkraut, as head dietitian, does not wear a company-issue apron. Nor does she wear a hairnet. Tall and thin in her high heels, Sauerkraut squeezes her long fingers around her hipbones, displays the precise match of her body-hugging dress and her slate-coloured nail polish.

"You've only been here three months. Do you realize what kind of message you're sending?"

"There is no message," Nellie shrugs. "If I wanted to convey deep significance, I would have written, 'Western Sandwich Big kaiser. Lots of ham. Egg in the background.' Now that warrants interpretation."

Sauerkraut raises her eyebrows slightly before pointing towards the kitchen.

"Stop interpreting and start splitting the kaisers."

Nellie's mother comes over to the cafeteria in the afternoon. The company subsidizes its employees' meals and snacks. Although Florence Mannville works for another oil company located several blocks away, she defects for Nellie's cheap coffee.

Flo and Nellie sit at a table at the front of the cafeteria. Flo glances at the daily special.

"Monday, June 1, 1998. Weevil Sandwich?"

"Western Sandwich," Nellie says.

"That doesn't work. Not like 'Macaroni and Feces'."

"Sauerkraut vetoed that one. And made me clean the tilt-skillet."

Florence lights a cigarette, cupping her hands around the lighter as though she is protecting the flame from a wind. "The landmans' golf tournament is coming up," she says. She peers over her glasses, exhales a jet of smoke. "I'd rather stay by myself at the office and bond with my own asshole."

"You'd miss the beer cart."

"I have work to do. I gotta figure out a way to pull some partners into this well we're drilling."

Flo pushes her shirt cuff up to her elbow, then lifts her cup in the air as Sauerkraut walks by their table. "Any more of this shitty coffee?" Flo calls to Sauerkraut.

Sauerkraut raises her chin and skims through the cafeteria to the kitchen.

Nellie wheels clean trays from the dishwasher room to the cafeteria entrance. She begins to load the trays onto the pop-up server.

"Your mother's a gas," Sauerkraut stops to comment. "Not many like her around anymore."

"Sixty-five-year-old female landmen who refuse to golf?"

"No, no. I mean smokers. Foul-mouthed smokers."

After work Nellie stops at the computer store. She hums a country tune, rocks heel-to-toe in her sturdy cafeteria shoes.

"Here it is," says the woman, setting a computer on the counter. "Sorry for the delay."

"I'm good at waiting. Did you fix the e-mail problem?"

"We couldn't find anything wrong. We couldn't even find the mail item you described."

Nellie picks up the monitor, shifts it to one arm so she can open the door.

On the way to her bus stop Nellie cuts through a parking lot. Each space has an electric outlet for plugging in car block-heaters during the winter. She stops, balances the computer on a curb stop, unwinds the cord, and plugs it into the outlet. On the screen, in a serif font, the same message appears:

> I have a bossy uterus. That's why I decided to work in the petroleum industry.

Nellie tugs out the plug, wraps the cord around the base of the monitor.

Computer on her lap, squeezed between other home-goers on the bus, Nellie faces the screen. She calmly watches the e-mail message slowly disintegrate into silver fragments, then blackness.

"Here, get with the nineties," Flo had said, setting the computer on Nellie's kitchen counter. "Something for your new job at the cafeteria."

"What will I do with that?" Nellie asked from her corduroy beanbag chair.

"I don't know. Recipes? You're working at a big oil company. Everyone needs a computer."

"I don't start until next week. They're not going to give me recipe homework. Thanks, but you should take the computer back."

"Keep it. It was just hanging around the office."

"I don't need it."

"Of course you need it. Just like you need all this

other stuff I've given you." Flo pointed around Nellie's main-floor one-bedroom apartment. "The futon couch, the iron coffee table, the beanbag chair, the bookcase, the bookends in the bookcase." Flo picked up one of the bookends and weighed it in her hand. The bookends were four-inch thick well core samples, sandstone, that had been cut on the diagonal to make two wedges. Flo slid the bookend back into place and said, "Even the books used to be mine. Before they were outdated. Energy regs, couple of old acts, CAPP binders, CAPL binders. Good Christ, look at this." Flo tipped a faded pink book out of the case. *And Baby Makes Three: The New Mother's Manual.* A nosy oil scout gave me this when I was pregnant with you." Flo shoved the pink spine back into position.

"So I'm not a shopper. Why unearth new stuff when this old stuff is right here under my nose, ready for use."

"It has nothing to do with shopping. It has to do with buying. You're not a buyer."

"Okay, I don't buy much. That's what makes me open to alternatives. I never close the door with a purchase."

"That's what makes you a mooch. Now take the computer."

"I'll try it in my bedroom."

Nellie cranks a can opener around a No. 8 size tin of pineapple tidbits. Sauerkraut flaps a sheet of paper in front of Nellie's eyes.

"Looks like you and I have to go on a rig tour next Friday," Sauerkraut announces. "Every new employee, it says here."

"How will a rig tour improve my fruit salad?"

"The execs think we'll be happier and more productive if we see where the company's bread and butter comes from."

"Grain crops? Dairy farms?"

"You know what I mean. Oil and gas wells."

"You're not a new employee. Why do you have to go?" Nellie asks as she sticks her fingers into the can to remove the lid before it sinks into the yellow juice.

"Something always comes up. I've missed it every year. Don't lick your fingers."

Nellie reverses the direction of her hand and wipes it on her apron.

"And Nellie," Sauerkraut clenches her teeth, "the memo says 'dress casual.'"

"What does that mean?"

"It means," Sauerkraut snaps the paper and lays it on the counter, "cowboy clothes or golf clothes."

Nellie holds her wrist with one hand, opens and closes the fingers of her other hand.

"The electric opener should be fixed by this afternoon. Watch out for repetitive stress," Sauerkraut says. She holds out one hand, analyzes her nail polish. "Cowboy or golf. I'm revolted by the choice."

Flo shows up at the cafeteria just in time for Nellie's mid-morning coffee break.

"A rig tour!" Flo snorts from her seat. "How will that help you chop onions? Never in your life have you wanted to go to a rig with me. Not even when you were working at that crappy drive-thru and a little road trip would have been the perfect getaway. Besides, I can tell you all you need to know in twenty minutes."

"My break's only fifteen minutes."

"The bigger the rig, the deeper the hole. Think of a dick. That's the derrick. At the top there's the crown. One-third of the way down there's the monkey board. Near the base there's the drill platform. On the drill platform there's the office or doghouse. On the ground there's the water tanks, mud tanks, mud-mixing shack, pump house. Drill a hole, hit petroleum, bring it in, pipe it away. Done." Flo slaps her palm on the table.

"Free breakfast and lunch on the tour," Nellie says, raising her coffee to her lips. "I'm going."

Nellie pushes through the revolving doors and into the main floor of the company tower in downtown Calgary. Employees steer past the giant bronze of a cowboy riding a bucking oil barrel, towards the elevators and their offices, or towards the escalator for a morning coffee at the second-floor cafeteria. A fountain of water arcs over the statue and makes a splashy deposit in a shallow pool. At the edge of the pool sits a square-shouldered man in a navy uniform, a clipboard on his knee.

"Do you know anything about the rig tour?" Nellie asks.

"This is the meeting spot."

"And you're the bus driver?"

"Coach driver." The man points to the big windows that front the building. "That's it parked across the street. Load yourself."

"There's a concept."

The bus driver looks puzzled. "It's open," he explains.

"I'll say." Nellie pats his clipboard. "Nellie Mannville is present and ready to load herself."

On the other side of the fountain, Sauerkraut beckons Nellie. The batwing sleeve on her dress flutters.

"I see you've dressed cowboy," Sauerkraut says. She nods towards the crowd forming around the bus driver. "Just look at them. Shorts, T-shirts, even tank tops." Sauerkraut shakes her head, continues, "Not just new employees, but utter workforce neophytes. They have confused casual dress with company-time casual dress."

"Are you supposed to be cowboy or golf?" Nellie asks.

"I can't go on the tour. Something came up. A memorial service for my mother this afternoon. A surprise memorial service."

Nellie's big cowboy buckle pops open. She cinches her belt up a notch and fits the hook into a new position. When she looks up, Sauerkraut is gliding up the escalator to the cafeteria.

Nellie waits beside the fountain, taps her cowboy

heels on the slate floor. Tap, tap, tap. Like a keyboard. Nellie taps out the message that was on her computer this morning.

> Life's like that. Sometimes your uterus seizes all the blood from your head and then you can't do anything but obey. I believe that's the medical explanation. Same sort of thing happens to men. That's how that awful expression that your mother used to use, 'dickhead,' came about. I can't imagine what she would call someone under the influence of a bossy uterus. Well, maybe I can.

Nellie climbs two steps into the bus. From the middle to the back of the bus, tanned legs stretch through the aisle, ponytails swing sideways and backwards. Nellie chooses the second row across from the driver. Setting her jean jacket on the aisle seat, Nellie slides in beside the window and begins to eavesdrop.

"I think you should get married around twenty-five. Then do some travelling. I want to go to Venezuela. I wouldn't marry anyone who didn't want to go to Venezuela. Then have a kid when I'm twenty-seven."

"My sister-in-law was thirty-nine."

"That's way too old."

As the bus starts and stops through the downtown

traffic lights, the bus driver reaches for a cardboard box on his dash. He fumbles with the lid and takes out a doughnut. Setting the doughnut on his thigh, the bus driver says into his microphone, "Here's breakfast."

He holds the box out into the aisle. "Sugar, glazed, or sprinkled?"

One of the new hires jumps forward and grabs the box. The doughnuts circulate down the driver's side of the bus and then back up Nellie's side.

Nellie peers into the box. There are no doughnuts left. Only oily spaces and one battered bismark.

"The doughnuts always go first," the bus driver apologizes. "Must be something about the empty centres. The holes. Kind of whimsical, don't you think?"

"Bismarks can be whimsical too," Nellie says before she bites. "Nothing predictable about a bismark. You never know what's inside."

"I think they're all jam centres," the bus drivers says. "I've never seen any other kind."

Nellie wipes bismark dust from her lips. "You never know."

She watches out the window while the road channels them away from the oil-company high-rises, past four car washes, two soft-cloth, two touch-free, eight gas stations, three full-serve, two owned by the company Nellie works for, six car dealerships, and nine opportunities for a lube job.

The traffic lights become less and less frequent until the city thoroughfare becomes a divided highway. Green hectares of grain begin on the roadside and rise to the foothills. Bright yellow flowers dot the canola fields. Cattle graze across expansive ranchlands. Even in early June calves stray from their mothers' flanks.

Parked in a fallow field, near the barbed wire fence, a truck and speedboat set display a "4 $ALE" sign.

"I need some different wheels," says a voice from behind.

"That truck?"

"No, an suv. Brand new. And big."

"Sell your little hatchback?"

"Yeah, it doesn't hold enough stuff."

The bus turns onto a narrow gravel road. Closer to the fields now, Nellie watches a wobbly shimmer of heat rising from the crops. The driver turns off the air conditioning to prevent dust from being sucked into the bus. The interior of the bus heats up. Voices behind Nellie become cranky.

"How do you open this frigging window?"

"Maybe loosen that clip first."

"You try. I'm dying. I need air."

"It's stuck or something. Look, they've got theirs open."

The bus lurches to the side of the road, half in the ditch to make room for an oncoming tractor and its trailer of dust. Nellie tries to filter the air by taking quick, shallow breaths. She puts her arm on the windowsill. Watches the dust tip the hairs on her arm, coat the beads of sweat.

Beyond Nellie's arm, several fields away, a derrick projects from the flat shimmering fields. The top of the derrick is red. Bright red. The rest of the derrick is a tower, narrower at the top, of white girders. Nellie blows a tight stream of air onto her wrist. The coolness of her breath raises goosebumps on her arm, sends a shiver to her shoulders.

About halfway down the rig, the monkey board has been boxed in like a tree fort. Cables hang through the centre of the rig from the crown to the base. Outside the derrick, one cable is strung from the crown to the ground, another from the monkey board to the ground. Keeping her eyes focused on the perpendicular structure, Nellie raises her other wrist and blows. More goosebumps.

Nellie spots her company logo staked at the turnoff. The bus veers to the other side of the road in order to make the turn, then stops for a company pickup bouncing from the rig towards them. A man in beige golf shorts, logoed golf shirt, and steel-toed boots hops out of the truck and signals for the bus driver to swing open the door.

"Howdy," he yells, waving at a point beyond Nellie. "I'm W.C." Then he turns to the bus driver.

"Road's pretty rough. Rutty from this past rain."

"No problem," the bus driver says. "I used to work the rigs as a nipple chaser. 'Till I got tired of running errands."

The bus driver swings the door closed and W.C. clings to the dash as the bus jostles to the rig.

At the rig, Nellie joins her group around the baggage hatch. The air outside the bus is less dusty. Nellie looks over her shoulder at the rig. She takes a deep breath. Holds it a moment, tasting bus diesel, rig diesel, diesel grease. An oily film lubricates the grey-white grit in her throat.

The bus driver hauls boxes of coveralls and goggles out of the baggage compartment. W.C. disappears into one of the rig-side trailers but then returns, wearing a trim-fitting pair of logoed orange coveralls with "W.C." embroidered on the arm. He walks to the baggage compartment, signals the bus driver to move aside.

"Howdy," he shouts, like the first time, above the roar of the still-running bus. He points to the rig, saying, "Let's suit up and take a tour of that telescopic double." Then he begins distributing blue coveralls. He tosses Nellie a "Men's Small." She hands it back to W.C.

"I'll take a woman's medium or large, thank you," Nellie says.

"No such thing." W.C. tosses the coveralls back to Nellie.

"Sure there is. I'm such a thing."

"The overalls or the bus."

Nellie pulls the legs on. They are snug around her thighs and too long. She puts her arms in the sleeves and shrugs on the top portion. There is not enough material to close the zipper that runs from crotch to collar. She tugs the zipper up a few inches, barely covering the crotch of her jeans. The material will not meet any higher. Nellie is not fat, but her torso is bismark-shaped. She looks around. The rest of the group, including the bus driver, has begun walking towards the rig. Nellie sets her hard hat on her head, fits the arms of the goggles behind her ears, and follows the group.

At the base of the rig, W.C. directs the new hires to stand together for a group picture.

"All you greenhorns line up there, backs to the water tank."

Nellie joins the group.

"Are you really new?" he asks, pointing at Nellie.

"I'm thirty-nine."

"Slide in closer to the kids. Thirty-nine? People used to start with a company after school and stay there until retirement. Company loyalty. That's what's missing. The way people change jobs these days, they're like balls on a driving range. Bouncing all over the place."

Nellie steps sideways, attempts one more tug at the zipper on her coveralls. W.C. raises the camera to one eye and encourages everyone to say "mother lode."

He shakes the camera. "What's the matter with the goddam thing?"

"Lens cover," Nellie says.

After the photo, W.C. leads the group up the flight of stairs and onto the rig. Nellie hangs onto the vibrating railings. Her toes mash against her cowboy boots. The bottoms of her coveralls drag over her boots so only the pointy toes poke out under the denim hem.

Nellie follows the group, teeters in her boots as they pass two pounding engines, and steadies herself against a railing when they reach the mud tanks. In front of them, behind a short guardrail, a pool of tea-coloured water froths. Nellie pushes her way to the front of the group, looks into the tank. She watches the small fountain, the source of creamy bubbles, rising slightly, then ebbing, in the centre of the tank. She leans on the guardrail, taking weight off her compacted toes.

"Nice boots," the bus driver says into Nellie's ear as he sidles up beside her.

"Got them years ago. The saleswoman said to break the leather in by wearing them through a creek. I went through the Belly River near my apartment. My feet cramped so much I had to limp home barefoot."

"The Belly River's pretty shallow, at least for a geological formation."

"They softened over the years, but this rig's making them feel new again. Must be the heat and vibration. Causing a swelling. Do you feel it?"

"You betcha," the bus driver says hoarsely in her ear.

W.C. waves his arms for attention. The roar of the mud tank generators and floor motors obliterates his voice. He points to the tank, yells something, points up a short flight of stairs to the drill platform. Nellie watches W.C.'s mouth and hands. She grasps the railing and tries to swing her boot into the tank, feels a tapping on her wrist. Nellie looks at the bus driver. He shakes his head no. Nellie pulls herself up to the reverberating rail. A new hire asks about colloidal suspensions. Nellie can't hear the full question, and W.C. doesn't seem to hear the question at all. Nellie's hands and arms begin to shimmy, adopt the reverberations of the rail. She pulls away, presses her hands together, steadies her feet.

"We're in luck," W.C. yells, pushing past Nellie on the rampway. "They're going to make a trip." He glances back at Nellie.

"They're going to pull up the string, change the bit, and add a length of pipe. Are you coming, lady?"

"I feel a bit confined. Cramped. I'd feel better if I took off these coveralls and my boots."

"That's a new one. You're lucky they didn't make you wear steel-toed boots. Maybe you should've brought ear plugs."

Nellie steps back against the railing.

"What does W.C. stand for?" a new hire yells.

"Wildcat," W.C. winks.

Nellie follows the group up the short set of stairs onto the drilling platform. Two roughnecks in hard hats and dirty coveralls wait at the centre of the platform where the drill stem rises out of the floor. Using hand motions and shouts, W.C. directs everyone to stand on either side of the doghouse window so that the driller inside the doghouse can see the drill stem and the roughnecks. The driller has taken his arms out of his coveralls, so the upper portion of the coveralls gathers in folds at his waist. He wears a grey muscle shirt and waits at the control panel, prepares to operate the drawworks and the slips, the wedges that keep the pipe from dropping down the hole. The roughnecks bend their knees, grab the giant tongs that will hold the drill pipe.

Nellie stands beside one leg of the derrick. She closes her eyes. Shuts out W.C.'s gesticulating arms and inaudible tour-talk. Hears only the screech and clank of metal until the bus driver shouts in her ear, "Are you okay? You look flushed."

"I'm crampy," Nellie says, opening her eyes and studying the huge pounding engines on the other side of the platform. "Maybe it's the motors."

"I suppose you feel faint. Do you want to wait in the coach?" the bus driver offers.

"No, it's not the motors." Nellie leans her head back into the ladder that leads up to the crown. "The derrick." She looks up and repeats, "The derrick." The sun presses down. She absorbs on one side the heat of the engines and on the other the heat reflecting from the aluminum doghouse.

"This derrick," Nellie says, "is starting my motor." She lowers her chin and looks at the bus driver. He removes his hardhat and smooths his sparse hair towards the back of his head.

"Well then," he clears his throat. "Well then."

Nellie looks up the derrick. A sweat bead slides from her nape between her shoulder blades, to her bra clasp. Nellie lets her head roll back again, focuses on the tip, the crown. She presses a hand on the stuck zipper of her coveralls. Presses, then relaxes. Presses, then relaxes.

The roughnecks work without speaking. They disconnect every second length of pipe rising from the ground. The derrickman, working above on the monkey board, racks the double lengths of pipe in the monkey fingers.

Nellie looks at the palm of her hand as though a message has been transposed there. She hooks the heel from her cowboy boot onto the bottom rung of the ladder. Her foot vibrates with the ladder. Once more she lays her hand over the stuck zipper, over her uterus, and presses. This time she presses deep, deeper than fabric, deeper than skin. Her brow furrows with concentration.

With a jolt, Nellie reaches the same hand above her head, grabs a rung on the ladder. Hand over hand, as though guided by a persistent knocking, Nellie begins to climb the thirty-metre derrick.

Sweat trickles from her back and armpits, dams up in her bra and in her underwear elastic. She is not cooled by the open fly of her coveralls. Or by the open fly of her jeans, which has loosened with the motion of her climbing and which unfastens as she ascends.

TICK TICK TICK. The sound of Nellie's boots on the rungs becomes clearer the higher she climbs.

Over halfway up the derrick, Nellie reaches the monkey board. Pauses. Bends her upper body off the ladder. She looks at the horizontal beams, the monkey fingers, that make up the floor. Like a balcony with every second floorboard missing. The derrickman's boots shuffle as he guides a vertical length of pipe through the monkey fingers.

"Don't stop what you're doing," Nellie gasps.

The derrickman looks over his shoulder, squints. "What? What are you doing here?"

"I want to go all the way," Nellie catches her breath.

The derrickman readies himself for another length of pipe.

"Is this some kind of joke? I gotta work. I gotta pay attention."

"Do you hear anything?" Nellie asks.

"I'm just doing my job. Racking pipe." He glances at Nellie again. "Are you clipped into something? You're not even wearing a harness."

"Protection would be pointless."

"Hey!" the derrickman bellows over the safety rail towards the doghouse. "Up here! Get her out of here!"

"Don't muck this up," Nellie says. "I'm on the brink of something huge."

She grabs the ladder. Starts to climb again. TICK TICK TICK.

"Get back here, you dumb bitch," W.C. screams from the drill platform.

Nellie peers down at the upturned faces, at W.C pointing at her, at the driller standing at the door of the doghouse, at the gape-mouthed bus driver. Nellie winces, brings a knee up. She breathes deeply as though trying to work out a runner's stitch. She straightens her leg. Steps up a rung. Another step. Faster. Her hands clasping, her legs pumping.

Nellie reaches the red crown in nine minutes. Drenched. Flushed. Sucking in the derrick-top air. She flops off the top of the ladder and lies on her back on the small floor. Inhales. In one corner of the crown there is a flagpole. The flag at the end of the pole flutters slightly, then settles.

The crown is the size of a small bathroom. There are red guardrails on all four sides and, protruding through the centre of the floor, the top of a huge pulley. With one hand Nellie pats the spool of wire rope leading down the inside of the derrick. The spool groans, rolls slightly, sleepily. Nellie places her other hand over her uterus. She presses slightly, shrugs, lets her hand drop.

Nellie rolls onto her knees and peers over the safety rail. Far below, the mud tanks gurgle. The new hires are proceeding off the drilling platform, some already moving down the stairs to the parking lot. Like a police officer controlling traffic, the driller ushers them off the rig with hand directions.

Clank clank clank.

Nellie crawls to the top of the ladder and looks down. W.C., wearing a harness and clipped to a safety rope, climbs the ladder. Nellie watches the top of his head, the steady approach of his yellow hard hat. As he climbs past the monkey board, Nellie can see the sweat glistening on his beet-red neck.

"Put this on," W.C. grunts when he comes off the top of the ladder. He holds out a harness to Nellie.

"I'm scared of heights," Nellie says.

"Lady," W.C. says through his teeth, "you climbed up here like a bitch in heat. Now you're going down in this harness."

"I was controlled by uterine forces. It's different now."

"The goddamn harness. Or I'm pushing you off."

Nellie sits on the floor of the crown, says, "Push me off? Bet that's not in the safety handbook."

"Legs go through first." W.C. drops the harness beside her.

Nellie puts her feet through the leg loops of the harness. She slides the rest of the harness underneath her bum and fastens the buckle around her waist.

"You're tied in. There's a counterweight at the other end. Take a few steps down the ladder and let go."

Nellie crawls to the top of the ladder. Backs her feet

down the top two rungs. Stops. W.C. puts his boyish face close to hers.

"Have you any idea what this downtime is costing the company? Per minute? Per second?"

Nellie white-knuckles the top rung of the ladder. Her cowboy boots, two rungs lower, jitter up and down.

W.C. peels her fingers from the top rung. Nellie's upper body tips away from the ladder. Her boot heels, spinning neatly to the underside of a rung, take a few moments longer to release. At first, Nellie kicks and makes panicky grasps in the air. But then, as she looks down and up, evaluating her speed against the height of the rig, she opens her arms and fingers to the breeze of descent. Her legs dangle peacefully until she lands with a thunk on the drilling platform.

"You must have had bedrock for breakfast," the driller comments as he unclips her harness and signals all's-well to W.C. in the crown.

"A bismark," Nellie says. "I'm ready for lunch."

The other rig tour participants are already on the bus when Nellie gets on. They are silent, staring. Nellie waves and takes her seat. Once the bus turns off the bumpy lease road, she falls into a deep, relaxed sleep.

Nellie does not open her eyes until they pull into the parking lot of a small-town golf course. The bus driver announces that lunch will be served in the clubhouse.

"You're late," a permed waitress snaps as the rig tour

enters the clubhouse. "Your cold cuts have been on the buffet for more'n an hour."

The bus driver explains that there was an unexpected delay, an incident at the rig.

"My advice to you," the waitress says, "is to never let an incident get in the way of punctual eating. Don't blame me if you get the botulism." She walks back to the table in the far corner of the clubhouse and sits down with a foursome of golfers. They all stare up at the television screen, where a man in pleated pants tees up his golf ball.

Two tables are set with paper napkins and a glass of forks. Nellie sits at one. The rest of the group sits at the other table.

The waitress leaves the television to take their drink orders, pulls a thick order pad from the breast pocket of her blouse.

"Chop chop, let's go. I'm missing the Buick Classic."

Nellie orders a rum and Coke.

"Good choice. We have them on special all the time in honour of the coker down the road. Carbon coke, you know. You can smell the refinery on the ninth tee."

"And a glass of water," Nellie adds.

"Bottled?"

"Tap water's fine."

"It's a buck either way. Water's getting as precious as gasoline."

Nellie examines the buffet. She spoons potato salad and ham loaf on her plate. Adds a slab of jellied tomato salad. The buffet table is pushed against a wall and on the wall, behind the jellied salad, is a large photo of a woman in a Stetson. She wears cowboy boots, chaps, and a short jacket. All in white leather, all fringed. She stands on top of a ridge, looking down at a panorama of foothills, rivers, and wheat-stooked fields. Scrawled on one corner of the photo is the name "Babs Howard."

"Did you see the driller?" Nellie overhears. "He's going 'fuck fuck fuck' when he sees her climbing the derrick. He can't just stop, eh. He's flipping all these levers trying to get things set so he can get out of the doghouse and have a better view."

"I didn't see that."

"You didn't even notice her going up, you were so busy going, 'Oh W.C., W.C. what's the current rate of penetration?'"

Nellie takes a devilled egg, returns to her private table. A rum and Coke waits at her place. Nellie takes a few gulps.

The bus driver enters the clubhouse, unbuttons the top two buttons of his uniform, and slides a chair alongside Nellie.

"I haven't been to the crown," he confides as he sits down, "but I was sent up to the monkey board once. I didn't like the way it made me feel. There was no solid floor. Just monkey fingers. Like walking on a giant air vent. But I could see why another person might find it stimulating."

"There's a great picture of Babs Howard behind the jellied salad," Nellie says.

"You did seem stimulated. I heard one of those kids say your nipples were pushing at your coveralls like a couple of golf tees. High beams, our generation used to call them."

"My grandmother used to make jellied salad. Tomato aspic, she called it, until my mother ruined the name for her. Aspic."

"Drink? I can make you a more generous rum and Coke in the bus. Maybe I could find Babs on the bus radio."

"Dessert."

Nellie ponders the dessert tray. Date squares and brownies. And, sitting in a big bowl of water with a few floating ice cubes, little plastic containers of ice cream, the kind that come with tiny wooden paddles for spoons. The paper lid of one has become drenched, partially opened. Soft vanilla ice cream seeps into the icy water, spreads white tentacles. Nellie stands beside the bowl and eats her ice cream. W.C. enters the clubhouse.

"Hey W.C.," a new hire ventures, "I heard you once had yourself lowered down the rat hole so you could fetch your sunglasses."

W.C. smiles. Turns an empty chair around, and slides the seat between his legs before he sits down. He crosses his forearms on the chair back.

"Heh, heh. Word gets around. Too bad you all had to get off the rig today. Safety procedures when something goes wrong. Otherwise you could have had a look down the rat hole. The mouse hole, too. Right there on the plat-form. But we had to get off."

W.C. glares at Nellie.

Nellie waves hello with her ice cream paddle at him.

"You're under his skin," the bus driver whispers.

"No, just running tests. He's almost impermeable. His casing runs thick and deep. Generations deep."

W.C. turns back to his table of new hires.

"I was lowered into that rat hole by three sets of coveralls knotted together. In the old days," he says, "we made do with what was around. Initiative. Bet you don't learn about that at your city desks. Like when we'd drill into the Wabamun and the well would take a drink, we'd try to plug the leak with whatever we could get our hands on. Straw. Bran. Tampons. Golf balls, of course."

"Aspic?" Nellie interrupts. "W.C., you must try the aspic."

Nellie partially undresses just inside her door. In order to avoid her oval belt buckle jabbing into her stomach while she takes off her cowboys boots, Nellie pulls her jeans down to her knees, tugs off her boots, then steps out of her jeans. It is only early evening but, after the incident, and after several rum and Cokes, several ice creams, and the bus ride home, Nellie is ready for her nightgown. She leaves her pants and boots on the floor and, walking past, flicks off her bathroom light.

Nellie's bedroom is only big enough for a single bed, a closet, and, at the end of her bed, a small table with her computer. If she uses her computer, she has to sit on her bed.

When Nellie enters her bedroom the computer monitor lights up, emitting an effervescent square of silver into the dark room. Nellie bends over to look at the screen.

> That was quite a rig tour. Hah hah hah.

Nellie checks that the power switch is off. She clicks it back and forth to be sure, then heads for her kitchen, where she reaches for a box of Cheerios at the back of her cupboard. She pulls the cereal bag out of the box and holds it up to the light. Unrolling the top of the bag, she sniffs, shrugs, pours a layer of Cheerios onto a cookie sheet. After grating cheese on top of the Cheerios, Nellie slides the cookie sheet into the oven. While the cheese melts she returns to her bedroom, sees the computer screen glowing silver again.

> We didn't need fancy-pants telescopic doubles. Wood rigs. That's what we had. If they were good enough for Old Glory they were good enough for us.

Nellie pulls at a Cheerio in the corner of the cookie-sheet, discovers all the Cheerios have become interconnected and can be peeled off in one piece. Side-by-side little circles held together by cheddar mortar. Nellie sits on the corduroy beanbag chair. From one hand she dangles the cooling Cheerio slab. With the other hand she phones her mother.

"Who'd you say these e-mails were from?" Flo asks.

"Someone named Doodlebug."

Flo says, "You're not dealing with a doodlebug. Nope. That stuff about the bossy uterus, that sicko 'hah hah hah' laugh. You've got yourself a pervert."

Nellie dips her head, takes a bite from the bottom of the Cheerios slab. Flo asks, "What's that sound? Are you eating something?"

"Cheerios."

"Aren't those for babies?"

Nellie holds the mesh of cheese and Cheerios in the air. "I've melted cheese on them. You should see, it looks like an orthopedic car seat cover."

After the phone call and Cheerios, Nellie unplugs her computer and moves it to the bathroom. She sets it beside the sink, opposite the toilet, and plugs it into the razor outlet. Nellie's bathroom is painted black.

"I never heard of a black bathroom," Flo said the first time she used the toilet. "It's like sitting in a miniature oil tank."

"In the morning," Nellie said, "it's like stepping into a cup of coffee."

"Or looking up someone's asshole," Flo said.

"If you like," Nellie replied.

Nellie pours soup from the big kitchen vat into the serve-yourself pot. Earlier in the day she had written "Minions-only" instead of "Minestrone" at the top of the cafeteria wipe board in the spot reserved for the daily soup.

Nellie looks into the soup pot. She looks closer.

"Problem?" Sauerkraut asks, stopping to look over Nellie's shoulder.

"It doesn't look the same," Nellie says.

"The same as what?"

"As this morning, when I poured in the chopped tomatoes and onions."

"Well, it's been simmering for hours."

"Look at it. Algae, minnows, ferns—all manner of prehistoric life."

"You're not making fossil fuels, you're making soup. Did you use the recipe from my binder?" Sauerkraut asks, without looking in the pot.

"Yes."

"Then it looks exactly as it should."

Nellie carries the serve-yourself pot out into the cafeteria and sets it up beside the bowls, just before the cash register. The first group of lunch customers are picking up trays at the start of the cafeteria. Nellie returns to the kitchen. She stirs the soup remaining in the vat.

"Get on with it," Sauerkraut says.

"I put macaroni in," Nellie says.

"So?" Sauerkraut says.

"This is tubetti."

"Not a chance," Sauerkraut says. "We don't have any. It doesn't come in bulk."

"See?" Nellie says, holding the ladle above the pot.

"Macaroni," Sauerkraut says, already on her way to her office at the back of the kitchen.

"Tubetti," Nellie calls. "Fallopian tubetti."

Nellie rinses out her coffee cup and dips it into the vat. Bringing the cup back to her mouth, Nellie slurps down a bellyful of the red soup. She dips again.

"Nellie," Sauerkraut barks from the doorway to her office, "that was a filthy thing to do. Whatever were you thinking?"

"I was thinking about ice cream," Nellie sets her cup on the counter. "The kind of ice cream on the rig tour. How it was like spermatozoa. How it would naturally accompany this tubetti."

Sauerkraut nods to the cafeteria. "Short order. Get there."

"Especially since I burnt my mouth," Nellie says on her way through the swinging doors.

"How was the rig tour?" Flo Mannville asks as she sets her coffee down and takes a bite of her subsidized muffin.

"I saw a picture of Babs Howard on a ridge."

"In white leather fringes? I've seen that one."

"And I got pregnant."

"That is news. How'd you manage to fit a screw in? The mud-mixing shack? Been there, done that."

"There was no screwing involved."

"Who's the satisfied father?"

"There isn't one."

"Why are you making this so difficult? What reservoir lost its semen?"

"There isn't any semen."

"You're not pregnant. You're nuts."

Nellie leans back in her chair.

"I mean it," Flo says.

"I mean it too." Nellie drinks the last of her coffee. "I'm pregnant."

Flo looks at Nellie's coffee cup for a few moments, then asks, "Did you get the computer fixed?"

"Sort of," Nellie says as she gathers the two empty mugs, starts walking towards the dishwashing room. "I don't think there was ever anything wrong with it."

I'm no pervert. Trust your mother to come up with that one. It's me, Grandma. Grandma Doodlebug. You never called me that but I would have liked it. You just called me "Grandma," generic grandma.

Once I met another doodlebug, a big barn-door of a man, who preferred to be called a smeller. But I didn't smell. Though I sniffed, for effect, on occasion. And I used the props. The divining rod. Sometimes I fastened a canning jar full of fresh crude oil on my rod. Sometimes I even put a few streaks of crude oil on my face and told them I cut my divining rod during a full moon.

The drillers liked that witchy touch. That was before everyone fell into the science pot. But really, all I did was walk around until I felt a cramp. Like a menstrual cramp. And then I told them to spud right there under my feet.

The group photo of the rig tour participants appears the July 1998 issue of the company newsletter. Nellie, thickish and sweaty, stands at the end of the middle row. Her jean shirt and jeans protrude from her open coveralls. Her big silver belt buckle catches the sun, twinkles like a magic egg on her belly. Sauerkraut cuts the photo out of the newsletter and pins it on the kitchen bulletin board, beside the safety chart.

"Did you enjoy yourself on that rig tour last month?" Sauerkraut asks Nellie.

"It was orgasmic."

Sauerkraut examines the picture.

"I doubt it. Hard hat, goggles, coveralls. Just look at you."

II

"We're not going to call this a cafeteria anymore," Sauerkraut announces. She adjusts the satiny cowl neck of her shirt and continues, "'Cafeteria' sounds like something from the fifties. It connotes hospital or prison food. We need a name."

"I have a name," Nellie says. "Nellie."

"Well, you might want to think about changing your name, too. 'Nellie' is so bovine."

"How about 'Flo'?"

"Another milk cow. Anyway, there's going to be a company-wide contest for the cafeteria name."

Nellie stands at a counter facing the wall. She pulls a Kevlar safety glove onto her left hand, sets a potato on the chopping block.

"Couldn't we just think up something ourselves?" Nellie asks.

"The execs think not."

Nellie steadies the potato and reaches up to grab the long handle of the potato-wedger from the wall.

"A tall person would have more leverage here," Nellie says, pulling the handle down. The wedger blades slice into the potato. Nellie releases the handle, allows it to snap back to its upright position on the wall. Finger-width pieces of potato drop from the block into a water-filled basin.

"'Nellie's Deli,'" she says to Sauerkraut. "That's a name."

The next potato rolls out of Nellie's hand, tumbles to the wall. Nellie's stomach presses against the counter. She has to tiptoe on one foot, balance the other leg in the air behind her, to reach beyond her six-month girth for the rolling potato.

"'Belly Deli,'" Nellie says. She settles the potato into position and pulls the wedger down.

"Is the water in that bucket cold?" Sauerkraut asks, watching the pieces drop into the basin.

Nellie sets another potato, reaches up for the handle again. "Repetitive stress injuries are common in kitchen employees."

"After the potatoes, I need you to prep the short-order cold table," Sauerkraut says. "There's a new box of tomatoes in the cooler."

Flo Mannville blows cigarette smoke through a crack in Nellie's apartment window. Half of Nellie's apartment is below-ground. During the summer the window swings open like a door, the bottom of the frame skimming across the top of the lawn. It is December, however, and Flo can only crank the window open a few inches before it is stopped by the crusty layer of snow. She stubs the cigarette on the back of the window frame and, using her thumb and forefinger, flicks the butt into the snow. Flo closes the window latch, calls to Nellie in the bathroom.

"Do you remember when we were at that pathetic baby shower last year and that four-year-old arsehole was there? Someone asked him if he thought it was a girl or a boy in his mommy's stomach. He said, 'Babies don't grow in your stomach. They grow in your fucking uterus.'"

"He didn't say 'fucking,'" Nellie calls back, over the sound of her own pee.

"His name was Kevlar. Why would someone name their kid that?"

"Maybe his parents had a Kevlar canoe."

"Why not just call him 'petrochemical'?"

"Why not?"

"My point is this: you weren't like that boy when you were little. You aren't like him now."

Nellie flushes the toilet. She exits the bathroom, adjusting a length of elastic which protrudes from the waistband of her maternity pants.

"I know how most babies are made, and," Nellie gently snaps her waistband in place, "I know how this one was made."

Flo wags her finger at Nellie's waistband. "Nellie, you're driving too close to the edge."

Nellie wags her finger at Flo. "Then maybe you should get out of the trunk."

"What's that supposed to mean?" Flo blinks.

"Quit making assumptions. Get over yourself."

"Oh for Chrissakes. It's you I'm concerned about. Look at me, I'm the same as always."

"Exactly. Beer?" Nellie walks towards the fridge.

Flo pushes the bridge of her glasses with her index finger, answers, "A couple. It's Friday. I could use the buzz."

Jim "Buzz" Brody. The oil scout. In the only absent-minded moment of your mother's life, she hooked up with Jim Brody. She was rid of him in a jiffy, but it only takes a jiffy. I suppose she thought he was dashing. He had his pilot's license and an open-cockpit Chipmunk that he used to spy on tight-hole rigs. Good with a horse and binoculars too. Even disguised himself as a water truck driver a couple of times. Got shot out of a tree by a driller once. But he ended up with high blood pressure, low-slung pants, and a paunch. Just as well your mother dumped him before you were born. Okay, okay, you've heard this a hundred times. But I'll tell you something new, your mother told me that you were conceived on a pile of empty drilling-mud sacks. And that Jim Brody yelled, "Blowout!" when his swimmers cut loose. Maybe that's when your mother decided to dump him. Anyway, she didn't need a rabbit to tell her she was pregnant. Neither did I. Neither do you.

You should walk more. Eat some apricots.

After Flo leaves, Nellie makes gazpacho. She chops tomatoes, cucumbers, bell peppers. Adds extra tomato juice. She minces an entire head of garlic into the bowl. Adds several green onions. Vinegar. Piquant salsa. Worcestershire sauce. Tabasco sauce. Jalapeno sauce. Chipotle sauce.

She lets the soup gestate in the refrigerator for two days before spooning out an inaugural bowl on Sunday night. The aroma burns a path from her nose to her tear ducts. The soup itself courses from tongue to colon. Nellie eats a second bowlful. Another as a bedtime snack. Another for breakfast before work. By midmorning Sauerkraut has called emergency services. Two women from the Canadian Western Natural Gas Company arrive to check the cafeteria stove. They poke their wands near each burner, inside the storage shelves under the stove. They wear blue coveralls, vacuum meters slung over one shoulder like a purse. The meters attach to the wands with a thin hose. Checking for the leak, they run their wands alongside the ceiling pipes. Like Sauerkraut, they smell gas but cannot determine the source of the leak.

"Gazpacho," Nellie mutters.

"Pardon?" Sauerkraut says.

"Gazpacho."

"Gazpacho is never on our menu. No cold soups. Even in summer. I tried chilled vichyssoise once. Everyone complained. And on the menu board someone replaced the 'V' with a 'B'." Sauerkraut sighs. "Their immaturity knows no limits."

Nellie moves to the serving area while Sauerkraut and the gas company women circle the kitchen. Nellie polishes the lids on the bain-maries, dusts the salad-bar sneeze guard. Bends to wipe down the cupboards.

"Careful," Sauerkraut, coming out of the kitchen, warns. "I'm behind you, passing through"—Sauerkraut's eyes widen, then blink before she finishes with—"to the cash."

Nellie stands quickly.

Sauerkraut, raising the dark nails of her right hand to cover her nose and mouth, proceeds to the cash register, supporting herself on the fingers of the hand that she drags along the counter until she sinks onto a cashier's stool.

"I noticed your nails," Nellie says. "What do you call that colour? Aubergine?"

Sauerkraut stares at Nellie.

"Eggplant?" Nellie asks.

Sauerkraut's eyebrows drop, her eyes narrow.

"Purple it is then," Nellie says as she turns, pushes

through the doors and into the kitchen, passes the gas-women with their wands and vacuum packs, and heads down the short hall to the staff bathroom, where she enters a stall.

A click of stiletto heels. Tap water running into cupped hands, splashed on a face. The rip of the paper dispenser. Nellie, standing fully clothed in the stall, squeezes her bum cheeks together and peeks through the space above the door hinge.

"Nellie?" Sauerkraut says into the mirror.

"Yes, Ms. Crowt?"

"Is something the matter?"

"No."

"There is evidence that something is the matter."

"Nothing."

"Do you need some time off to see someone? Your doctor, perhaps?"

"Time off sounds good."

"Take the day."

"Ms. Crowt?"

"Yes?"

"How about 'Crowt's Combustibles'. You know, for the contest."

"I believe you mean 'comestibles'."

"No, combustibles. 'Crowt's Combustibles'—food energy to burn."

Sauerkraut smooths her hands along the sides of her narrow dress, pulls open the bathroom door, and says over her shoulder on the way out, "I'm sure someone will come up with a name, Nellie."

Nellie is the only passenger on her bus ride home. Stretching her legs far into the aisle, she uses her boots to scrape together a mound of winter grit and mud from the floor. Then she flattens and squares the mound into a slate-like surface. With the toes of her boots she begins to doodle.

Every so often, at a stop, the driver twists around, rests her elbow on her knee, and peers down the aisle. After turning around several times the bus driver squints under the seats, sniffs. "Do you smell a rotting onion sandwich coming from back there? It wouldn't be the first time."

"Don't see one," Nellie replies. "But I've been busy drawing a small, yet competent, oval. And here's my tall isosceles triangle. Also competent. Now, if I balance the oval on the very tiptop of the triangle, I make a little person."

The bus driver tugs at her side window.

"Darn thing never opens. Squirt of WD-40 would make it slide."

Nellie doesn't bother going into her main-floor apartment. Instead, she follows a path around the building to the long flat garage that contains a space for each tenant's vehicle.

Nellie pulls up her garage door and gets into the driver's seat of her baby blue 1968 Chrysler Imperial convertible. The Imp. A hand-me-down from her mother.

Not only is the Imp too long for most downtown parking spaces, it is a tight fit in Nellie's garage. When she backs the Imp out, Nellie cannot crank the steering wheel until the front bumper clears the garage frame. By that time, the back bumper is centimetres from the fence across the alley.

Horizontal baby-blue scrapes mark the bottom half of Nellie's garage door frame. The fence directly opposite Nellie's garage is splintered inward. The sides of the Imp are pocked with rusty scars.

Nellie's garage neighbour, Bitumen, owns a pipsqueak Firefly. Bitumen has strung a golf ball from the roof of her stall. The Firefly is in the perfect centre of the stall when the dangling golf ball touches the windshield.

Nellie swings up her garage door to see Bitumen just getting out of her Firefly.

"No work today?" Bitumen says to Nellie.

"Day off to buy a bigger bra and some bigger underwear."

"Don't get a front closure. Better to have the three-hook expansion-option of a back closure if you're overeating."

"I'm pregnant."

"Then don't get an underwire. That will ruin your milk."

Nellie opens the Imp's door, begins to duck under the convertible's retractable top.

"Bend forward and let your breasts fall into the cups. That's the way to get a good fit," Bitumen says over the roof of the Firefly.

"What is that?" Nellie points to a plastic cup-shaped object hanging from the Firefly's rearview mirror.

"My pump protector. For the heel of my clutch foot.

Driving a standard is murder on snakeskin shoes." Bitumen walks around her car to Nellie. She pulls up the leg of her grey flannel pant to reveal a scaly shoe. "I use an oil-based emollient to keep them from molting."

Once Nellie has maneuvered the Imp out of the garage, she drives down the back alley and pulls into the corner service station. While the pump jockey, a teenage girl in red coveralls, squeezes gasoline into the Imp, Nellie buys a bag of beer nuts from the convenience store and returns to the driver's seat. Numbers click by on the pump.

Nothing wrong with gas. It brightened a lot of prairie towns. Did I ever tell you, I suppose I did, that I was in Calgary in the summer of 1912 when they brought north the gas from Old Glory. Eugene Cost orchestrated quite a demonstration. The papers said 15,000 came out to watch. All dressed up like they were going to a United Church bazaar. When Cost's men opened the control valve, a cloud of dust and stones and wood splinters roared out. Mrs. Cost was trying to shoot a Roman candle at the entrance of the six-inch pipe. She had a pannier skirt and the most startling hat, a white straw hat big as a Mexican sombrero, with what looked like a heap of chickens piled on top. She hit the pipe end on the fourth shot and there was a terrific explosion followed by a sheet of flame at least a 100 feet high. I don't doubt that Mrs. Cost filled her muslin drawers. If I was older I might have suffered heart failure. But I was only a teenager.

When the crowd surged back I gave the big lout in front of me a crack on the back so that he wouldn't go stepping on my boots. Those boots never did wear-in properly. The saleswoman sold me a size too small. Told me the leather would break in. I was too young to know better.

We got used to the flame but the noise was deafening. I heard that an outgoing train had to send a walker to nudge people off the track. We couldn't hear the whistle. I couldn't hear clearly for days. Not that I needed to. My uterus always spoke loud enough to me, and all those wildcatters down south paid me dearly for the information.

The Imp takes a long time to fill. Nellie has almost finished the nuts by the time she prepares to leave the station. She sticks the key in the ignition, turns the engine over, puts the Imp into gear, all the while holding the long tubular nut bag up, trying to shake the last few nuts into her mouth. Nellie steps on the gas pedal.

I never ran a car. Ned owned one though. Maybe because he hailed from Turner Valley where everybody wanted a Buick as big as their boss's. Ned knew a fellow, Nitro Charlie, who had a Buick roadster. Charlie came up from America to shatter the rock at the bottom of a few wells. In front of the rear wheel of his Buick he had a special compartment, sort of a trap door, for his golf clubs. He used the rumble seat for a drum of nitroglycerin. Bounced all over Turner Valley with that drum six feet from his head. Ned thought Charlie was a hero. I thought Charlie wanted attention.

In those days, you could see the gas in the pumps at the service stations. Visible pumps, like gumball machines. But the pumps were for tourists and newcomers. Ned just drove up to the Dingman well site and helped himself to a pail of natural wet gas. There was always a pail of naphtha for those in the know.

Nellie slams on the Imp's brakes, glances behind her. She pulls the gearshift, rolls the car forward a few feet, and gets out to survey the damage.

The pump jockey jogs toward the Imp.

"Is it bad?" the girl asks.

"Crinkle cut," Nellie says, pointing to the uniform dents in the Imp's bumper. She has backed into three upright, bright blue pipes, each one taller than her, that rise out of the pavement.

"Those are the breather tubes from the gas reservoirs. I have to make a report," the girl says. "And phone the police. For insurance purposes."

"I'm going home," Nellie wipes beer nut dust from her thighs and settles back behind the steering wheel, "to get some gazpacho."

"You can't go. They'll need your statement."

Nellie closes her door, rolls down her window, and says to the pump jockey, "Tell them I was forward thinking but backward driving."

The pump jockey reaches for the car door.

Before the girl's fingers touch the handle, Nellie steps on the gas, calls out the window, "Tell them that it could have been worse. I could have been trying to drive from the trunk."

Although the company employs hundreds of people, only five entries are made in the "Name Your Cafeteria Contest." Sauerkraut, along with two junior geologists and one summer student, is on the judging panel. She shows Nellie her notes.

Rigs and Buns: rejected. Limiting description of foods provided.
Catalyst Cafe: rejected. Suggests unwanted intestinal reactions.
Fucking Shitty Food Place: rejected.
Derrick's: Pros: drilling structure, first name of company CEO.
Cons: CEO eats at Petroleum Club, not cafeteria. Plus, CEO hopes to be transferred back to head office in US ASAP.
Doodlebugs: winner.

"Congratulations," Sauerkraut says. "You have a car, don't you?"

She hands Nellie the envelope that contains the prize for the winning name—a fill-up of high-octane gas.

"A Chrysler Imp."

"Impala?"

"Imperial."

"I love a truly big vehicle. What year?"

"Sixty-eight."

"Ooh-la-la. Now that's sexy."

"Doodlebugs?" Florence Mannville says, looking up at the new wood-burnt sign dangling over the cafeteria entrance. "Did you enter that name? Some sort of whacked-out memorial to your grandmother?"

"It beat 'fucking shitty food place,'" Nellie replies, nudging her mother. "I know your work when I see it."

"That contest box was just sitting there every day I came for coffee. I had to enter something. I had to stuff something into that slot. Or steal the box."

"I believe you. Black Gold or Zama Roast?" Nellie asks before picking up the coffee pot.

"Gold."

Nellie fills Flo's cup. Flo takes a few quick gulps while they stand at the coffee pot, before they pay, then slides her cup back towards Nellie. "Fill 'er up."

Nellie tops up her mother's cup. They proceed to the cash register where Nellie receives a twenty percent employee discount and pays for both cups. At their usual table, Nellie sets her coffee down. Florence looks at her hands while Nellie lowers herself into the plastic chair.

"If I can accept your urge to 'stuff or steal' the contest box, why can't you accept what's going on with me?" Nellie asks.

"Because I need proof."

"Doesn't my size constitute some proof?" Nellie pats her belly.

"No. That could be due to lots of things. Maybe a combination of overeating and premenstrual bloating. It will right itself and you'll be fine in no time."

"I'm fine right now. It's you I'm worried about."

Nellie laces her fingers, twiddles her thumbs.

"Great, just great." Flo shrugs and reaches for her cup. "Can we drink our goddamn coffee now?"

"Favourite part of my day."

"Mine, too."

> I've been surfing on your behalf and discovered that a pregnant woman shouldn't consume angelica, barberry, black cohosh, celandine, dong quai, lobelia, pennyroyal, rue, or tansy.
>
> Sounds like a list of names for milk cows, if you ask me. Who keeps these things in their larder?

On Christmas Day Nellie drives over to Flo's house. She parks on Flo's driveway and walks up the short footpath to Flo's one-story sandstone house. A few small bushes, surrounded by cedar chips, are under Flo's front window. In the centre of the front lawn is a huge fir tree. Flo opens the heavy front door.

"Ready?" Nellie asks.

"Shall we take my Jeep?" Flo points to her garage door, then presses a small control box in her hand. The garage door opens. Nellie steps back along the footpath. Flo follows her.

Nellie looks at the glistening vehicle inside.

"What happened to your car?"

"Sold it yesterday. Bought myself a Christmas present."

"I thought we weren't going to buy presents this year."

"For each other. The deal was too good. I practically stole this little sport utility vehicle."

"No doubt."

"I thought you'd like this. There's no trunk for me to think in," Flo opens the driver's side door and sits behind the wheel.

"There's a hatch. Same thing, almost." Nellie turns towards the Imp.

"Aren't you coming?" Flo asks from inside her new Jeep.

"I've left the Imp running, we may as well take it."

"What if it snows, are you still sporting those bald tires?" Flo taps her foot on the running board.

"It's not going to snow today."

"Why not? It's December."

"Because it's eleven degrees. If anything, it will rain."

"Rain on Christmas. In Calgary. Whoever heard of such a thing?"

"Climaglobologists. They says it's the warmest year of the millennium. I saw buds on the poplar trees the other day."

"Climaglobologists. Don't try to hoop me. You just made that word up, didn't you?"

"Yep." Nellie opens the Imp's door for her mother.

"Do you remember learning to drive this car?" Flo pats the Imp's dusty dashboard.

"I didn't want to learn," Nellie says, settling into the driver's seat.

"I never understood that."

"I was only nine years old. The Imp was brand new."

"Never too early. We were driving to Waterton to go camping. Your grandmother was in the back seat. We stopped at a gas station and I got in the passenger seat while you were in the can. Then when you came out—surprise—you got to be queen of the road."

"But I didn't want to drive a car. I wanted a bike. A banana seat bike."

"We sat beside those gas pumps for what seemed like hours. Your grandma had a handful of rock candy in her mouth. Cracking and slurping. Sounded like someone boring under a riverbed. Drove you so crazy you finally stepped on the gas."

"I don't remember Grandma eating candy. I remember you cleaning your glasses over and over again on the tail of your shirt."

"And that's when you found out that the Imp doesn't just accelerate, it rockets. Passengers, adjust your headrests."

When your mother was ten I bought her a rock polishing set. She took pebbles off the street and put them in an electric tumbler with grains of sand. As she poured in finer and finer grains of sand the pebbles transformed into gemlike stones. That Christmas your mother gave me an earring and necklace set made from the rocks. They were speckled blue and green. Remarkable. I wish I'd been buried in them instead of the fake pearl get-up someone scrounged from my jewellery box.

When your mother was eleven, she traded that rock-polishing kit for a go-cart. I think the go-cart must have been worth more since it had a two-cylinder combustion engine. Somebody got a bad deal.

Nellie and Flo drive the Imp to a restaurant at the city limits. They park in a lot beside the restaurant. The sky is black, night-cloud covering the moon, but the semi-trailers parked farther down the lot glisten. Their stream-lined air foils reflect the string of blue and red Christmas lights around the restaurant.

"They've renovated since last year." Flo shuts the Imp's door.

"Put in showers for the truck drivers." Nellie slams the Imp's other door.

"They've got the Christmas decorations out."

Flo and Nellie cross the parking lot and stop for a moment at a display on the small patch of grass in front of the restaurant.

"How old is that plywood nativity scene? Fifteen years?" Flo asks.

"Older. Ever since we've been coming."

"It's a wonder that duct tape has held Joseph's head on for all these years."

"A miracle." Nellie looks sideways at Flo.

Flo pulls open the glass door and, with her hand, motions Nellie through. "Turkey special with giblet gravy?" Flo asks.

"Stewed tomatoes," Nellie says, passing through the doorway, "and maybe some apricots. With steak sauce. They always have a bottle of HP in the trolley with the salt and pepper and sugar."

Nellie and Bitumen sit at the kitchen table in Nellie's apartment.

"I've come about the incident," Bitumen says.

"At the drilling rig? That was months ago."

"At the Premium Gas station."

"Oh, that was nothing. Now the rig incident, that was something almost inconceivable. Almost."

"My client, Premium Gas, naturally expects some reparation of damages to the air pipes. And, of course, they are still owed the amount of the gas. With interest compounded at a semi-annual rate."

"I thought you worked in a lingerie department."

"I decided to become a lawyer. It's easier than re-boxing bras."

Nellie shrugs, asks Bitumen, "How much do they want?"

Bitumen leans back, puts her palms on the table, "A gazillion dollars."

"I see," Nellie nods.

"I knew you wouldn't be phased by the amount. You're not the type. By the way, it will be more than a gazillion if we go to court."

"I'll think it over, Bitumen."

"Bitu. I'm going by Bitu now."

"How do you spell that?"

"Bitu, as in *in situ*, but with a 'B'. Here's my card," Bitu says, laying a small rectangle of paper on the table.

Nellie picks up the card, slides a corner between two bottom teeth inside her mouth.

"Must be a tomato seed stuck," she mutters while Bitu closes the clasps on her briefcase.

After Bitu leaves, Nellie walks her fingers along the spines of Flo's old energy regulations and binders in her bookcase, over a faded dictionary, moves down a shelf and stops at *The New Mother's Manual*. She opens the pink-cloth cover, flips pages until she reaches the back where, on the multi-lined page titled "Mother's Notes," there is one handwritten entry: "January 23, 1959, Nellie born. Home from hospital in '59 Pontiac Laurentian." Nellie turns to the section of the book on determining due dates, reads that an average pregnancy lasts ten lunar months. Nellie pulls the dictionary out of the bookcase and looks up "lunar month."

Your mother was always good at making deals. Go-cart deals. Land deals. She's done well for herself. And for you. Of course, they only write oil books about the million-aires. About the gushers. About the men.

III

Flo rushes into Nellie's hospital room. Nellie lies on the bed, her eyes closed, her face blotchy and flushed. Flo gently shakes Nellie's shoulder. Nellie's eyes flutter.

"I came as soon as I got Sauerkraut's message," Flo says. "I've been looking all over for you. They didn't have your name at the information desk."

Nellie yawns.

Flo continues, "I just knew this pregnancy-thing was going to end in the hospital."

"What's that crying?" Nellie asks, blinking.

"You're right across the hall from the new baby nursery."

"Oh yeah. Is there still a sandwich in here?"

Flo looks around the room. Walks to the other side of the bed and picks up a sandwich tightly wrapped in plastic film. She unpeels the film, hands the sandwich to Nellie. Nellie props herself up on one elbow and takes a bite.

"Little apricot jam might have been good," Nellie says after swallowing.

"In egg salad?"

"To each her own."

"Yuck. So tell me the story. Did the doctor give you anything?"

"Just the sandwich. I didn't need anything."

"Sauerkraut made it sound like you were unconscious."

Nellie pulls her hand from under the sheets, uses it to cover her mouth during another yawn.

"I was unloading clean trays of coffee cups from the conveyor and stacking them on the dolly," Nellie says. "There was a meeting going on in the cafeteria and this woman asked me to close the door to the dishwashing room to keep down the noise. So I did."

"Did you give the paramedics your pregnancy line?"

"I was in a faint on the floor," Nellie says, taking another bite of the sandwich. "I gave them my horizontal line."

"Must have been the humidity from the dishwasher," Flo says.

"Mom, it's not the humidity, it's the heat." Nellie stretches.

Flo rolls up the plastic wrap until it is the size of a golf ball.

"Petrochemical. Polyethylene." Flo displays the crinkly globe in her hand. "The oil industry has come a long way."

"Definitely the heat, the sudden warming in dishwashing climate," Nellie says, watching Flo arc the plastic across the room.

"Hole in one," Flo reports when the plastic lands in the garbage can.

"You're not listening," Nellie says.

"I'm listening and dismissing. It's a useful skill I've acquired during my career."

Nellie props herself up on her elbow. "I'm talking about global warming. Right there in the dishwashing room."

"Well," Flo leans toward Nellie, "unless Sauerkraut was serving toasted fossil fuel sandwiches for lunch, there was no increased greenhouse effect in Doodlebugs. You just got hot. Your body's gone through a lot of changes lately."

"The heat in there could have melted a polar ice cap," Nellie says.

"A few degrees can make a difference. Maybe you should get your hair cut short," Flo suggests. "Like mine."

Nellie runs her fingers through her shaggy hair. "Nah, my hair's okay. It's not affecting my health."

I could have made a tidy sum during World War II. It takes a lot of fuel to run a war. Everyone worried about petroleum reserves. I had an American officer come knocking on my door one morning, wondering if I was available for a little doodlebugging in Norman Wells.

"Ma'am," he said when I told him I had no intention of getting on a plane, military or otherwise, "it's about the war effort."

"Mister," I said, "it's about my effort. I don't like heights. I don't like flying. Especially with an outfit that believes Norman Wells is in Alaska."

He came back two more times that week. He knew I was one-of-a-kind. The first time he came back he brought a little nurse doll for your mother. Starched cap, navy cape. The last time he brought me a lace sack full of pull-taffy. He said he made the candy himself. I put that pull-taffy in the icebox. The next day, when I opened the door to have myself a sweet, the nurse doll was sitting in the icebox with the empty lace sack on her head.

I didn't worry about the taffy on your mother's teeth. She was twelve years old and had molars like millstones.

It drove Florence crazy when I

called the refrigerator the icebox.
But that didn't stop me from saying
it. Icebox. Hah hah hah.

A nurse pushes a woman in a wheelchair through the doorway. The woman in the wheelchair holds a swaddled bundle in her arms.

"Sorry," the nurse exclaims when he notices Nellie and Flo. He begins to back the wheelchair out of the room, "they told me this bed was free."

"I'm just leaving," Nellie says, pushing down the covers and then swinging her legs over the side of her bed. She is wearing the too-tight maternity sundress she wore to work that morning. Overtop she is still wearing a bibbed Doodlebugs apron.

"Isn't this your room?" Flo asks, looking at Nellie's bulging leather loafers. "You've got your shoes on."

"It was an empty room. After they checked me out of emergency I thought it would be a good time to test things out."

Florence called Norman Wells a
refrigerator. She went up once. After
Christmas. At Christmas we always
had a real tree, a Douglas fir, in the
sitting room and we always stood it
in a tri-cone bit. Drill bits made
marvelous stands. That year I gave
Flo some socks and a stack of bright
dickeys for her neck. You were a

teenager. You gave her a steamy terrarium. I didn't want to hurt your
feelings at the time, but all that
steam indicated that the terrarium
climate needed adjustment.
Florence returned in such a hurry,
she didn't bring your terrarium or
my dickeys back with her. Just left
them in some Atco trailer up north.

Flo and Nellie walk by a string of bathrobed women using the pay phones. Flo taps the down arrow for the elevator. Every few moments she pushes on the bridge of her glasses with her index finger. The elevator doors open and Flo and Nellie step in.

"I have to stop at the pharmacy on the first floor," Flo says. "I'm getting a headache."

"Maybe your glasses need adjusting," Nellie says.

"My glasses," Flo turns her face from the numbers above the door to look squarely at Nellie, "are well-adjusted."

"I should get some petroleum jelly."

"What for?" Flo asks, pushing again on the bridge of her glasses.

"External use only. The pink *New Mother's Manual* said I should slather my nipples with petroleum jelly or cocoa butter."

Did your mother tell you that she
had to come home from Norman

Wells because I hurt my back shovelling snow? I did. That was a real winter. Snow to the eaves. Do you remember how it used to snow? I loved shovelling. Thank goodness you weren't the type of girl who cared if the neighbours saw your grandmother shovelling snow while you listened to your records inside.

I could take care of me. You could take care of me, in a pinch. Your mother came home because she took a company vehicle, a half-ton six-wheel truck, to the bar. Like everyone, she left her truck running the whole time she was tipping drinks. But unlike everyone, Florence's truck ran out of gasoline. Must have got herself in some altered state where she believed her gas tank was unlimited. It wasn't. So there she was, last out of the bar, tight, with a frozen company vehicle.

They sent her home. Florence said it was worth it to see a woman in the bar eat a beer glass. Why would anyone do that? Why would Florence want to watch?

Flo snatches a container of Aspirin from the shelf and checks the expiry date. Nellie wanders down the baby-product aisle. She picks out a large jar from a shelf and takes it to the pharmacy desk at the back of the store. A pharmacist in a white lab coat stands at the counter.

"What exactly is in petroleum jelly?" Nellie asks, holding up the container.

"Let's see." The pharmacist takes the jar from Nellie and looks at the label.

"Petroleum, I guess." The pharmacist hands the jar back to Nellie. "I read somewhere that petroleum jelly was discovered by roughnecks."

Nellie shrugs. "Petroleum jelly just doesn't sound as tasty as cocoa butter. Although I like the idea of jelly."

"What do you need it for?"

"My nipples, mainly."

"Thank goodness," the pharmacist pats her chest in relief. "For a minute I thought you were going to eat it. I don't think they recommend cocoa butter for nipples any-more. Anyway, we don't carry it."

"Is this the biggest container of petroleum jelly you have?"

"That's pretty big."

"So are my nipples."

"I could order an industrial bucket for you. Four litres. But it might take a couple of weeks to get here."

"I'm good at waiting," Nellie says. "Order me a dozen."

Maybe it was Florence's molars

grinding that beer glass. Her breath certainly was gritty when she arrived home, leaned over my bed, and tried to get me to go to the hospital to get my back checked. I told her, "If you make me go to the hospital I'll tell Nellie you lost your job because you were tight."

I don't regret telling you this. Not one bit. I was pronounced dead at the Supreme Gas station, in front of a string of outdoor vending machines. Why didn't someone take me to a hospital then? I may not like hospitals, but when it came to a death setting, who wouldn't take a hospital over a gas station? How do you know that my soul isn't still bobbing around the gas bays like a grand-opening balloon, kept aloft by exhaust drafts and oil fumes?

In the parkade underneath the hospital, in her Jeep, Flo takes the headache medication out of the paper bag and pops off the lid. She shakes two pills into her hand and slams them into her mouth like peanuts. She leans forward to turn on the ignition, stops.

"If you were going to have a baby you would have had one by now." Flo leans back in her seat, looks at Nellie.

"Plain and simple. It's been a year since you started this production."

"There will be a birth scene," Nellie smiles.

"Don't hold your breath," Flo starts the Jeep.

"Of course not. That would be counterproductive."

"This whole situation is counterproductive," Flo speaks over her shoulder as she backs the Jeep out of its spot. "Totally fucking counterproductive."

"You're right," Nellie nods. "We should get out of the trunk. Look for alternatives."

"Fine." Flo brakes, pulls the gearshift into drive. "You start, Nellie. What's your alternative to this pregnancy thing?"

"This pregnancy," Nellie says as she presses the switch that locks the doors, "is already alternative."

IV

Flo and Nellie sit at their usual table at Doodlebugs. Flo taps her butane lighter on the top of her cigarette package.

"This has gone too far," Flo says. "I've made an appointment for you with Dr. Cost."

"What for?"

"Someone should look at you. I mean a medical person. Please. I used to be mad but now I'm worried. Do you want me to talk to Sauerkraut? I'll drive you to the appointment in the Jeep."

"This is not a case of bad menstrual cramps in junior high school, Mom. I'm forty years old. If I feel like going, I'll get there myself. I know how to get time off. Gazpacho."

"Are you sure? Dr. Cost is busy—if you miss the appointment it won't be easy to re-book."

"I have to pee."

"I'll take that as a yes." Flo relaxes into her chair back. "Dr. Cost's been busy since she opened shop. The great-granddaughter of Eugene Cost, founder of the Western Gas Company. Think of the goodwill attached to that name, eh?"

Nellie rises from her chair. Her belly knocks the cafeteria table and Flo's coffee wobbles, spills down the side of her mug.

"You'll never get in again this winter," Flo steadies her coffee. "Dr. Cost is a busy snowmobiler."

Nellie looks out the window to the grey street below, then turns and begins to walk across the eating area to the bathroom.

"It doesn't matter that there's no snow downtown," Flo calls after her. "There might be lots in the mountains. Dr. Cost could find snow in a desert."

"Deserts are getting bigger," Nellie calls back.

"Oh, the global warming thing. That's not proven, you know. Besides, Dr. Cost could still find snow."

I didn't know Ned at the time, but he was one of the boys hired to dig the pipeline from Old Glory to Calgary. Every so often I borrowed a horse and rode south, doing a little exploratory doodlebugging. There was plenty to cramp about.

There were two crews building the pipeline. One started in Calgary and worked south. The other, Ned's crew, started from Bow Island and worked north. They laid and welded all 170 miles of pipe in just 86 days. That was a feat. The horses hauling the pipe should have got a medal.

I would have remembered Ned if I had seen him back then. Even though he could sink a 6-inch stake with two licks of a sledgehammer, Ned was poultry-chested. Like your mother. Not like you and me—we've got big lungs.

Nellie reaches across the pasta salad container for the plastic wrap.

"Watch out Nellie, you're going to get yourself wet."

Sauerkraut points at Nellie's chest. Nellie straightens up, looks down the front of her Doodlebugs apron. Since Nellie can't tie the back strings, the apron dangles loosely from her neck.

"There," Sauerkraut points, "some dressing, beside your apron, on your blouse." Nellie picks up the hem of her apron and wipes at the creamy white smear on her breast.

"Don't you have any support?" Sauerkraut asks.

"Labour support?"

"Full-figure support."

"I got tired of upsizing." Nellie manipulates her right breast with her left hand, searching for more salad dressing.

Sauerkraut winces, asks, "Maternity clothes too small?"

Nellie releases her breast, drops the hem of her apron. "Yep."

"Then perhaps this is not a maternity matter," Sauerkraut sighs. "It's been eighteen months. You could've had two children by now. Two well-fed children."

"I've been thinking about thong underwear. My neighbour, Bitu, says they're an easy fit. Good for an ungainly figure."

"Ungainly?"

"That's what they call it in the pink manual I've been reading."

"I hope there's a chapter in your manual on the value of presentation."

"Headfirst is easiest, and most common," Nellie confirms, "but some are breech."

"You know I didn't mean presentation of the baby during birth. You're trying to get me going down another track. I was talking about the importance of visual detail. The high-heeled shoe underneath a scalloped skirt. The diamond brooch on the black gown. The cherry on top of a parfait. The . . ."

"Flag on the rig," Nellie interrupts, sealing the plastic wrap around the salad bowl.

"Put that on the bottom shelf so no one mixes it up with the other pasta salad in there," Sauerkraut says, watching Nellie walk toward the cooler.

"The flare at the refinery," Nellie calls as she opens the cooler latch.

"The wacko in the kitchen," Sauerkraut mutters.

"Heard you," Nellie sings before she enters the cooler.

Nellie drives slowly in the lane beside the meter-parked cars. A bicycle courier thumps the Imp's hood with her hand, then pulls in front, shaking her fist. Nellie circles the block, pulls into a loading zone. Before she turns the engine off, a honking semi-trailer, covered with advertisements for bottled spring water, pulls up to the Imp's rear bumper. Nellie turns a knob on her dashboard, pushes *Babs Howard's Gigantic Hits* into the eight-track stereo. The semi nudges her bumper, blares its horn. Nellie hums along with Howard's cracking voice. The Imp moves forward in short jolts as the semi bumps her out of the loading zone. Forced into the flow of traffic, Nellie puts the Imp into drive and enters a parkade. Looking for a space, Nellie winds her way up the parkade, and then, scraping her way down the ramp, tries again. This time she parks in a designated handicap space on the rooftop level.

In Dr. Cost's office, the receptionist seems surprised by Nellie's answers to her questions.

"You haven't seen a doctor yet? How far along are you?" the receptionist asks for the second time.

"Eighteen lunar months," Nellie answers. "And I have seen one doctor. That was in emergency about six months ago."

"Was that about your, ah, pregnancy?"

"No, it was about a dishwashing accident."

The receptionist picks up her pen, asks, "A cut?"

"No," Nellie sinks into a chair in the waiting area, "an environmental matter."

"So you haven't had an ultrasound?"

"Just an ultra pregnancy."

The receptionist smiles and sets down her pen.

When Ned started ditching for the pipeline, the rest of the crew had already been working for a few weeks. On Ned's first day, during the dinner break, some of the fellows told him that since he was the newest member of the crew he had to walk over to the farmhouse and get the apples. The crew told Ned that the farmwife had a stash of sweet apples in her root cellar. They said the farmwife admired the hardworking crew and always set aside a sack of apples for the workmen. So Ned followed the fenceline to that pretty house and knocked on the back door.

The door swung open and Ned said the woman behind it looked like a canister of nitro about to blow. Ned asked her if there were any spare apples about. I'm sure he took off his cap and asked politely.

"The only apple I'd give you is a road apple," the woman said. She meant the kind dropped by live-stock.

Turned out that woman's brother and sons worked at the Lethbridge coal mine and none of them liked the idea of a natural gas industry. Turned out Ned was the third worker sent to that woman's house in as many days.

Nude in the examination room, Nellie waits.

She flips through pamphlets on osteoporosis and breast examination. Takes a handful of Q-tips from one of the jars. Tucks the Q-tips, one by one, under her right breast, walks to one end of the room and back. No Q-tips fall to the floor. Nellie reads the label on the tube of PAP-test lubricant. She pulls one of the Q-tips from underneath her breast and uses it to clean her ear. As she switches the Q-tip from one ear to the other, she looks out the window.

From the examination room window, many floors above the rooftop parking space, Nellie watches a little red tow truck back up to the Imp's crinkled bumper. A minia-ture couple, the woman in a scarf and the man in a fedora, stand near the bumper. The man shakes his aluminum cane at the Imp. The cane is shaped like an offset putter.

Nellie tosses the yellow-ended Q-tip in the garbage slot under the sink. She unscrews the lid of a glass jar and grabs a handful of tongue depressors. She places the tongue depressors under her left breast, then paces back and forth, pumping her arms like a power walker. The tongue depressors and the Q-tips remain in position. Nellie stops at the window.

The tiny man takes off his hat and hands it to the woman. She holds the fedora as though it is a fragile aspic. The man raises his cane above his bald head and swings it down. The cane bounces off the Imp's trunk. The woman nods, allows the man to clasp her elbow while they shuffle to the corner of the car and the man sidearms his cane into the Imp's tail light. Moving in slow, shaky steps, he heads for the front.

Nellie holds her breasts away from her rib cage and lets the Q-tips and tongue depressors fall to the floor. She pulls on her caftan, her winter boots, and a poncho she has made out of a four-point Hudson's Bay blanket. Grabbing the large tangle of scarlet elastic from the paper-covered examination bed, Nellie hurries out of the room. With the hand holding the scarlet thong, Nellie waves goodbye to the receptionist.

Flo gives Nellie a ride to the car pound to retrieve the Imp.

"Whooooeee!" Flo says as Nellie closes the door to the Jeep. "Don't light a match in here. We'll have the biggest butt flare in history."

Nellie pulls the seat belt to its full length and snaps it into the buckle.

"Are you still making that gazpacho?"

Nellie stares at the red light in front of them.

"So what did Dr. Cost say?"

"Nothing."

"Nothing? What kind of doctoring is that? She's breathed in too much Ski-Doo exhaust."

"The receptionist mentioned an ultrasound test."

"Ultrasound? On you? That's like shooting seismic in a black hole. What's the point?"

"What do you know about black holes?"

"I know that whether its ultrasound or seismic, there has to be something, a structure, for the waves to bounce off."

"Some black holes are pink."

"Yep. Sure." Flo says to the rearview mirror.

"Ask an astronomer."

Nellie opens the glove compartment and takes out one of the many packages of buffalo jerky that her mother keeps in case of winter stranding.

"Can you turn off the heat?" Nellie asks, using her teeth to open the jerky package. "My feet are sweating."

"What are you wearing snow boots for?" Flo asks, peering at Nellie's feet.

"Habit. It's December."

"They're hardly necessary. The streets are clear. No snow. No ice."

"What are you driving a 4 x 4 for?"

"It's not the same thing."

At the car pound, both Nellie and Flo attempt to pry the aluminum cane from the Imp. They yank up, they push down, they try a jiggling motion. But the bottom of the cane is wedged, just near the front of the car, in the crack formed by the hood. The hood will not open and the cane, which protrudes a horizontal metre from the front of the Imp, will not budge.

"You may as well go back to work, Mom."

"What are you going to do about the cane?"

"I'll just leave it there. My vision won't be affected."

"At least tie a long vehicle warning flag on it."

Nellie knots her scarlet thong on the protruding handle of the cane, pays her fine at the car pound office, and guides the Imp onto a large road that leads out of the city. Once fixed on a straight highway north, Nellie cranks up *Babs Howard's Gigantic Hits* and steps on the gas.

Two-lane highway. Undulating prairie. Uniform rows of black troughs and mounds in the fields. Silver-tarped bales built into rectangles the size of the entire garage behind Nellie's apartment building. Nellie passes a group of horses at a fenceline, scraggly winter hair around their faces. A few dairy farms. Beef cow and calf operations. And, almost every quarter section, Nellie sees a mechanical oil pump bobbing to and from the earth.

When you were little you were always rolling down your window so you could get a clear view of the Herefords. You liked the patterns on their coats. "I'm not slowing down for a bunch of docile, plain-faced cows," Florence would say. But if your mother saw some Charolais, well, that was a different matter altogether. "Look at 'em," Flo would say. "Big. Bold. Strong. In-your-face cows." And when she spotted a Charolais bull, well, she pulled over on the shoulder of the road so she could complete her admiration.

But as you know, that is if you ever listened to the voice in the back seat, the most important thing about cattle is not the size or coat colour, it's their ability to calve. No deliveries, no cattle.

On the roads we travelled with Florence, there were almost as many mechanical oil pumps as Herefords. "Steel mosquitoes," you'd call out if you saw a field of them. "Pump jacks," Flo would say. And then I'd call out "horse-head pumps" while I cramped up in the back seat.

Nellie turns off the highway and drives toward the tall flare stack, topped by a gas flame, of the gas plant. When she reaches the plant she drives around the outside of the chainlink fence, past the buildings and the office trailer. The ground inside the fence is cleansed gravel. The buildings are white. Nellie passes the short lengths of pipe that deliver the gas plant's excess heat to the greenhouse. She drives through an opening in the fence and parks at the greenhouse, under the air vents and giant fans.

More than a year ago, when Nellie was barely showing, she met a gas plant operator. He operated a much smaller plant than the one Nellie is at now, but it was the same concept—to make the gas from the wells marketable. A couple of times a month the operator drove in to the Calgary office for meetings. On those Calgary days, he ate at Doodlebugs. Nellie met him when she was on hot-table duty.

"Make sure you have some meat pre-sliced for the rush, two thin slices per person, and no more than an ice cream-scoop portion of mashed potatoes and vegetables. Our budget depends on portion control," Sauerkraut said.

"Where's the ice cream scoop?" Nellie asked.

"Eyeball it," Sauerkraut said to Nellie.

Nellie eyeballed a pale man across the counter. The operator. She forked two slices of ham onto his plate.

The operator pulled a tissue from his pocket and wiped his forehead.

"Fever?" Nellie asked.

"Hormones," the operator wiped the back of his neck.

"I hear you." Nellie heaved another scoop of peas and carrots on the operator's plate and pushed the plate across the service counter.

"For the same price as the special?" he asked, looking over his shoulder.

"I know hormones," Nellie said.

The operator was blockaded before he paid. Sauerkraut, working the main cash that day, picked the plate off his tray, leaving only a small milk and a goblet of banana pudding, and carried the plate to Nellie.

"An explanation?" Sauerkraut set the plate on top of the service counter.

"Too many vegetables," Nellie admitted.

"No, this," Sauerkraut pointed to a tiny pink fold between the ham slices. She inserted her long cobalt-coloured nail between the slices and pulled back the top slice.

"Is that a Band-Aid?" Nellie's eyes widened.

"That's what I asked myself at the cash," Sauerkraut said.

"It doesn't look used," Nellie said.

"Unacceptable." Sauerkraut crossed her arms.

Later, Nellie restocked the drink cooler, warm drinks to the back. Carbonated pop, carbonated juice.

"I would have eaten all the vegetables if I had gotten my plate back," the operator said as he knelt beside her.

"Too bad about the ham." Nellie opened a cardboard crate of diet pop.

"I don't eat ham, anyway."

"I eat ham. But not Band-Aids."

"Do you take coffee breaks?" the operator asked.

"The bathroom in my apartment is like a coffee break," Nellie said.

The operator blushed.

Ned. You always bothered me about him. When we met he was a tool-dresser on a cable rig. I never told you that. Your mother turned "tool-dresser" into a dirty word. Ruined it for me. The old cable rigs, jar heads we called them, pulverized the ground. Punched their way into the formation. Sometime you should try lifting the chisel at the end of the cable stem. That was Ned's job when we met. He changed the mother hubbard chisel.

We worked as a team for a while. I divined oil, Ned punched it out. We stayed friends. That's more than I can say for some parents. (Not that your baby will have to worry about that. Hard to fight with an inanimate father.) Look at Florence and Jim Brody. Oil and water. Ned was a good man and would have helped me out, if I'd needed any help. As it happened, I had your mother in '33. I recovered quick and my doodle cramps started with my first walkabout. There was oil to harvest, but no money to pull it out, no capitalization, the drillers said. Ned couldn't find work anywhere so he decided to go to one of Prime Minister Bennett's unemployment relief camps for single men. The men cleared the bush for 20 cents a day at those camps. I was going to give Ned $10 as a send-off present but, when I pulled my change purse out at the train station, the bills had gone missing and there were only coppers left. There had been more than $25 in there. But the paper money had disappeared. Lord knows how. All Ned got was a peck on the cheek from me and a lot of shrieking from your mother. Maybe she was wet.

There's always been money floating in my teacup. And sure enough, a few days later all that money turned up inside one of Florence's little sleeping suits. Kind of odd, that. But she wasn't yet a year old; she couldn't even walk. You'd have to believe in tall stories to believe that she took the money. No, I think Ned put the money there so as to avoid an awkwardness at the train station.

*Ned was a fine man. But your mother
and I got by swimmingly without him.*

During one coffee break at Doodlebugs, the operator
drew flow diagrams on napkins.

"To get the sweet gas we have to dehydrate the raw
field gas." He tapped his pencil on the napkin. "This is a
glycol dehydration unit."

Nellie gulped the rest of her coffee. Lolled her head
from side to side to stretch her neck.

"We have a 1000-horsepower two-stage reciprocating
compressor."

Nellie peered into the operator's Styrofoam cup. He
always took his coffee in a Styrofoam "to go" cup.

"The engineers are worried about the dew point
climbing," the operator muttered.

Nellie pulled the Styrofoam cup towards her and
picked at the rim, crumbled the cup down to a miniature
bowl.

"Have I shown you my pigs?" The operator pulled
his wallet from his back pocket and flipped it open to a
photo holder.

Nellie leaned across the table.

"These are my utility pigs, I call them my Durocs."

His index fingernail, a perfect moon and smooth,
squared-off nail, hovered above a picture of a stack of
small plastic canopies. "Different sizes for different pipe
widths. They're for cleaning, separating, dewatering, that
sort of thing."

Nellie nodded.

The operator turned to a picture of a tightly threaded string of plastic doughnuts, steel doughnuts, and circular brushes. "These are my Lacombes. Inspection pigs. They tell me what's happening in the pipe."

Nellie held up her hand while she studied the photo. The operator waited a moment, then turned to the next photo.

"And these are my unconventional gel pigs, my optimizers. Swallow Bellied Mangalitzas, I call them," he said about the clear beakers containing neon-coloured gel. The operator's fair skin became a continuous blush. "They're the joy of my life."

Nellie took the wallet from the operator. Slowly fingered through the photos.

"How do you manage them all?" Nellie murmured.

"Oh they just sit around, except when I blow them through pipeline sections."

"I had no idea."

"Those pictures are out of date," the operator said. "The herd has changed a lot over the last year."

"There's a phone call for you, Nellie," Sauerkraut calls from her office one afternoon.

Nellie sets the big pickle jar on the cooler shelf, closes the latch as she exits the cooler, crosses the kitchen into Sauerkraut's office. Nellie picks the phone receiver off the desk.

"Hello?"

"Nellie," the operator speaks softly, like a golf commentator. "This is it. We're pigging."

Nellie glances at Sauerkraut.

"This is Nellie Mannville," Nellie says into the phone.

"The tech back at the plant has started a Swallow Bellied Mangalitza with a solid-cast Duroc caboose. I'm down pipe a couple of kilometres. I'm going to put the phone to the pipe. You and I should be able to hear the pig at the same time. Exactly the same time."

Sauerkaut opens the drawer underneath her desk. She pulls out a tubular object the size of a thick pen. An electrical cord dangles from one end.

"That would be fine," Nellie says.

Sauerkraut leans under her desk and plugs the cord in. The tube starts to buzz.

"The pig's coming any second, any second. I'm putting the phone on the pipe now," the operator whispers.

Nellie closes her eyes, strokes her neck.

Sauerkraut spreads her fingers, braces her hand on her desktop. With her other hand she picks up the buzzing tube, holds it like a pen.

"I'm ready," Nellie says.

"YES!" the operator screeches.

Nellie strokes her neck a few more times. She opens her eyes. Clears her throat. Looks at Sauerkraut.

Sauerkraut presses the end of the buzzing tube on the unpainted nail of her index finger. She buffs quickly and efficiently, working her way across each nail to her pinky finger.

"Did you? Did you hear it squeal past?" the operator asks.

"Yes. Thank you for calling." Nellie puts the receiver into its cradle.

"Generally, I do this at home," Sauerkraut says, laying her thumb on the edge of her desk in preparation for a buff, "But I just haven't had time."

"I didn't notice," Nellie smacks her lips and pats the phone.

"The electric nail buffers are so much better than the old emery-board style. It's easy to do yourself. I'll let you borrow this during your coffee break if you want. Buffed nails will make you feel better about yourself."

"I can't imagine feeling any better than I do right now," Nellie says over her shoulder as she leaves Sauerkraut's office.

Inside the gas plant greenhouse, tomato plants brush Nellie's elbows, exude a tangy smell. Nellie's sunglasses fog up. She hangs them on her caftan collar, continues along the cement pads to the office at the back. Nellie knocks at the office door, waits, then walks towards a rustling in a nearby aisle. Nellie peers through the plants, sees a figure crouching at the base of the plants in the next aisle. Stepping over hoses, squinting in the reflective light of the greenhouse, Nellie strolls up the aisle, then down the next aisle.

"Any tomatoes for sale?" Nellie asks.

The woman at the base of the tomato plants turns her head.

"Bitu?" Nellie asks.

"I'm going by Bitty now. Be with you in a minute." Bitty wears gumboots, a sweatsuit. She pulls a water spike from the base of a plant. Waits for a drop of water to fall from the end, then reinserts the spike in another position. She looks at Nellie's feet.

"You shouldn't be wearing winter boots in this weather," Bitty says as she stands up. "Even if it is winter. There's no snow. You'll wear down the soles on the pavement."

"Anything happening on the Supreme Gas case?"

"All my files are in the Firefly. I should pass them on to another lawyer now that I'm working here."

"Where's your Firefly? I didn't see it parked out front."

Bitty stands, points to a corner of the greenhouse where the white roof of the Firefly protrudes like a block of salt.

"Part of my contract. You've got to negotiate these things up front. Indoor parking, coffee breaks, proper balance in the air of oxygen, nitrogen, carbon dioxide, water vapour, methane. Life's little luxuries."

Nellie inhales. "Bad air at the law firm?"

Bitty nods. "Bad air, good parking. It was a trade-off. I quit to come here when fashion took another polyester turn. All the labels on my business clothes were from designer petrochemical companies. The petrochemical industry is taking over the world. You should quit your job so you're not part of the conspiracy."

"If there's a conspiracy, this greenhouse is part of it. Any tomatoes for sale?" Nellie asks.

Bitty holds up a triad of small green tomatoes. The slim leaves at the top of the tomato all point towards the transparent ceiling.

"I thought they'd be ripe by now," Nellie says.

"Nope."

"I'll get some anyway."

"Look at my watch."

Bitty cocks her wrist to emphasize her thick, scaly watchband. "This is an ideal environment for reptilian fabrics." Bitty's hand drops. "You should get a job here. Then you wouldn't have to take the bus to work. You could drive. There's lots of parking space here for the Imp. And you can wear snakeskin."

"Nothing wrong with the bus. Except it doesn't have an eight-track player for my Babs Howard tape."

"See, everything's a trade-off."

"I have to go," the operator said at their last meeting. He slid his forefinger around the rim of his Styrofoam coffee cup, tilted his head slightly. "They're sending me to pigging school in Texas."

> I've heard a pig. A real pig. Not some polyurethane petrochemical multi-tasking gimmick. In my day they were only for cleaning.

Ned sometimes worked as a pipeliner. When the volume was down and the pressure was up we knew something was blocking the line. So we wrapped barbed wire around a bundle of straw and pumped it through the pipe. Now that pig squealed. Barbed wire scraping against the inside of the steel pipe. The sound made me want to squeal. The fellas at the pig trap end, where the pig finished its journey, said it looked like an overdone pork roast when they took it out. Greasy, black, and perfectly shaped for a fancy serving platter.

The operator set a large rock in front of Nellie. On the rock face was a fossilized spiral-shaped animal. In the centre of the spiral was a clock.

"I'd like you to have this before I go," the operator said. "It's an ammonite clock. From the Bearpaw formation. Well, the fossil is from the Bearpaw. The clock is from Sears."

"I'm a Mannville formation," said Nellie.

"I think," continued the operator, gliding his fingertips along the top of the rock, "it represents an intriguing visual and metaphoric link between modern time and geological time."

"Right now," Nellie said, "I'm more about biological time. Do you mind if I give it to my mother?"

Flo Mannville sits in Nellie's beanbag chair and drums her hands on her thighs.

"Sauerkraut phoned me at work today. She says you brought a carton of green tomatoes to work."

"Do you want some?" Nellie asks. "I've got lots left over."

"I see that," Flo says, raising her eyebrows at the tightly packed line of tomatoes on the window sill. More tomatoes line the back of the couch, the nooks of the bookcase, the kitchen counter, the headboard of Nellie's bed.

"Sauerkraut thought it was odd."

"I've got more in the bathroom, on the computer."

"Do you really think they're going to ripen?"

"Grocery stores buy them green."

"Grocery stores gas them to make them red. What are you going to do?"

"Wait. I'm good at waiting."

Flo wrings her hands together. Then she picks up a green tomato and passes it from hand to hand.

"Mom, did you ever use a rectal thermometer on me?"

"Oh for fucksakes, Nellie, is that what this is all about? Is this whole charade going to come down to something I inadvertently did or did not do as a mother? I hate that kind of story."

"I'm just curious. Look at this picture." Nellie pushes

a tomato aside, takes *The New Mother's Manual* from the book case, and flips to the page where a wide-eyed baby lies on its back on a change table. A woman's hand holds the baby's ankles in the air, at a ninety-degree angle to the table. In the other hand she points a thermometer at the baby's anus. The baby's short black hair stands straight from its head.

"Is this the sort of thing a mother needs to know?" Nellie holds the photo in front of Flo's face.

"The first thing a mother needs to know," Flo says, "is how to get pregnant."

"Mom. Please?"

Flo looks at the picture a little longer.

"Okay. I probably got your grandmother to do stuff like that."

"Probably?"

"I don't remember."

"Me neither."

Flo takes the open book from Nellie.

"You'd need a lubricant, something like petroleum jelly, for that sort of procedure," Flo decides, closing the book. "It's a grandmother's job. Any beer?"

Nellie shelves the book.

Flo knocks once on the door and steps into Nellie's apartment. "Nellie? Ready to go?"

"I'm not going to the diner," Nellie calls from the bathroom.

Flo crosses her arms. "What do you mean you're not going to the diner? It's Christmas. We always go to the diner."

"We don't have to do the same thing all the time. We used to stand a Scotch pine in a drill bit every year and we don't do that anymore."

"It was a white spruce. What's the matter with the diner?"

"I've got all these tomatoes here," Nellie says, flushing the toilet and coming out of the bathroom. "I can whip us something up."

"Let someone else do the whipping-up."

"The thought of turkey special makes me gag."

"Order something else. Have stewed tomatoes like last year."

"Just being in the same room with a turkey special is going to put me over. I can tell."

"Aren't we fussy all of sudden," Flo says. "The diner is tradition. We've done it for years and we should do it this year."

"Look outside," Nellie points to the window. Flo stays in the doorway with her arms crossed.

"If you don't want to go to the diner, why don't we go to the drive-thru. Eat in the Jeep. You could get a slice of tomato on top of your burger. Maybe you could say hi to some of the people you used to work with there. Although not everyone stays at that type of job for as long as you did."

"Look outside," Nellie says.

"Ketchup. You could ask for extra packets. Ketchup is made from tomatoes."

There is a brief spattering, like gravel, on the window pane.

Flo steps into the apartment, "What's that sound?"

Nellie points to the window. The apartment is silent for a few seconds. Then the dark, still window is pelted with bullets of almost-frozen water.

"Sleet? Whoever heard of sleet on Christmas Day?" Flo touches the window with her fingertips.

"I'll fry up some tomatoes." Nellie opens a cupboard.

"I'm parked out in the open. The Jeep's gonna get hammered. Maybe I'll have to get a new vehicle," Flo says. "Sleet damage. Maybe a Hummer."

"Tinsel with your tomatoes?" Nellie asks. "That will make it Christmassy."

"Maybe a sports car." Flo presses her palms together.

> Thermometer, shmermometer. If I could divine millions of barrels of oil in the Devonian formation at Leduc, don't you think I could divine a fever in a baby? Take my advice and worry less about the core temperature of your baby and more about the potential for sass— the likes of which your mother gave me. If I e-mailed her, she'd trash me. Thank God for grandchildren.

V

"I want what's best for you," Sauerkraut says to Nellie in the morning, while Nellie lines up cinnamon bun rows on a platter. "This is precisely the sort of thing that the disability plan is for. You've been paying into it. You'd be crazy, completely nuts, bonkers, not to take advantage of it."

"I feel fine," Nellie says. "No hemorrhoids, thank goodness. I've heard they're like having a chunk of conglomerate in your crack."

Sauerkraut leans towards Nellie, firmly whispers, "Hemorrhoids are a private and persistent form of rectal varicose veins. They are not a determinant of good or ill health. They are private."

"Well I feel pretty good without them." Nellie snaps her tongs in the air. Sauerkraut steps back, "You are not symptom-free."

"I have symptoms of pregnancy, not disability."

"You have symptom excess."

"As my mother says," Nellie shrugs, "go big or go

home. I'm going big. Physically and metaphorically.

Sauerkraut smiles. "After your disability assessment, you'll be going home. Literally."

Flo Mannville brings over a case of beer. On the sidewalk in front of Nellie's apartment, she crushes her burning cigarette with her runner and sweeps it with her foot onto the brown grass. Flo watches the sprinkler dribbling water on the centre of the grass for a moment, then picks up the butt in her free hand and carries it into Nellie's apartment.

"Don't want to piss off your landlord at a time like this," she says as she sets the beer beside Nellie's kitchen sink. "Don't want you without a place to live, too."

Flo looks around. It is early evening and the room is gaining shadows.

"Nellie?"

"I'm in the bathtub. Cooling off."

The bathroom door is open. Flo pulls the lid down and sits on the toilet seat beside the computer.

"It's still a scorcher out there. I never used to think of June as a hot month. What've you got in the water?"

"Oil. I got the idea from the pink *Mother's Manual.* There's a section on how to give a baby an oil bath."

Nellie splashes water onto her belly. Massages the oil around her belly button. "Mind you," Nellie continues, "they recommended it for tiny and delicate babies. That's hardly me, and I doubt it will be my baby. But it feels good on some of my friction spots." Nellie smoothes her hands along the inside of her thighs. The loose flesh pillows in front of her hand.

Florence peels the brown paper off her cigarette butt and pulls at the tuft inside.

"Tow," she says. "Cigarette tow."

Nellie looks at the shredded filter.

"They make it up in Edmonton," Flo continues, faster, "from natural gas. Bet you didn't know that."

"Nope." Nellie picks up a plastic bottle from the edge of the bath, dribbles baby oil across her collarbone.

"Just making conversation," Flo shrugs.

Nellie squirts a stream of oil into the water.

"Never trust a woman who treats her fingernails like pets," Flo says.

"Sauerkraut's all right."

"All right?"

"It's not like she fired me."

"What's the difference? She doesn't want a barrel-shaped psycho working in Diddlybugs."

"Doodlebugs. And I'm not psycho. I'm pregnant."

"Here we go." Flo stands, lifts the lid, tosses the cigarette butt into the toilet. Nellie bends her legs, begins to push up on the sides of the tub. Her feet skid back towards the drain.

"Pretty slick," Nellie says.

"Need a hand?" Flo asks.

"Not yet." Nellie lies back in the tub.

In the history books, everything is always Leduc, Leduc, Leduc. Time according to Leduc. Pre-Leduc. Post-Leduc. Yackity yack. For everyone in those books, Leduc meant money. For me, Leduc meant dry skin and sweat-soaked sleeps. I was menopausal. Worse, I was ignored. Those new boys thought a doodlebug needed explosives and geophones and recording trucks and seismograms. So now they've got all that clutter. And still drill dry holes all over the place. Their technique is like tapping on drywall, listening for a different sound, a joist. Except each tap costs a barrel of money. Where's the efficiency in that? I may have been menopausal by the time they finally started drilling in Leduc, but my doodlebugging uterus was right as rain.

Flo flushes the toilet. The ceiling bulb flickers, then lights the room with a steady white beam.

"Didn't you get this light fixed?" Flo asks.

"It was never broken."

"I didn't touch the switch," Flo holds her hands out, palms up. "Listen, the computer's starting up, too. You've probably mucked up the wiring by putting the computer in the razor outlet. What's the computer in here for anyway?"

"I'm pregnant. I spend a lot of time in here. My wiring is fine."

"Some, like Sauerkraut, think otherwise," Flo tosses a towel onto Nellie's oily belly.

"Now," the company nurse asks, "you've been pregnant for how long?"

"Twenty-four months," Nellie says.

"Twenty-four months," the nurse bites her lower lip for a moment. "Starting to feel a bit uncomfortable?"

"Not bad," Nellie says, readjusting her body in the chair. She slips off a shoe, holds up one thick leg. She traces a few circles in the air with her foot.

"When do you expect this baby?" the nurse asks.

"Couldn't be too long now," Nellie says. "Look at how petite my foot is."

The nurse nods several times.

"Soon I'll have tiny pointed feet just like the new mothers in *The New Mother's Manual*," Nellie says, sliding her toes back into her flat loafer. "Proportionately speaking."

The nurse supports her clipboard on her forearm. She writes quickly, with solid-sounding i-dots and periods.

"Get many pregnancies through here?" Nellie asks, working her heel into her shoe.

"Mostly just allergic reactions to Friday morning doughnuts."

"We don't get doughnuts in the kitchen. Unless we buy them."

"Here's a Canada Food Guide. Why don't you have a look at it while I fill out these disability forms."

"I don't recall doughnuts being on it," Nellie says.

Leduc No. 1 was a wildcat. They were guessing when they drilled. Few people expected anything. Except me. I walked the lease long before they spud the well, and with the biggest series of contractions I'd had since Turner Valley, my uterus divined a huge underground reservoir. Sure as sugar, February 13, 1947, there was about five hundred of us, in our fur coats and wool toques, waiting for the coming-in ceremony to start. It took a while, since the swabbing unit broke, but in the late afternoon a gurgling mix of oil and gas and drilling mud spewed out of the pipe and into the flare pit. Your mother and I were standing in the front row near the flare pit. We watched a piperacker tie a rope around some sacking. Then he poured diesel fuel over the sacking and felt around the pockets of his overalls. He asked if anyone had a match. Your mother

produced a box of Eddy matches
out of the pocket of her dungarees.
She tossed them to the piperacker.
He shook a match out of the box,
lit it by running the sulphur end
across the seat of his pants, then
held the flame to the sacking. The
sacking caught fire and the piperacker swung it, lariat-style, into
the end of the pit. Whoosh. The pit
lit up and a perfect smoke ring
sailed into the air. Even the piperacker was surprised by that smoke
ring.

"Now, sweetie," the company nurse says, "don't you worry about coming in to work. I'll send a community nurse right out to your place. I know a good one who has a minivan and will keep me up-to-date. So don't you worry about a thing."

Nellie looks up from the Food Guide. "You've got me wrong. I don't worry. I adapt."

Once a week a nurse, appointed by the company nurse, comes to Nellie's apartment in a white minivan. He knocks lightly at the door in the same tap-tippy-tap-tap rhythm. Nellie is slow to answer the door so he begins again. Tap-tippy-tap-tap. Nellie opens the door after he deletes the "tippys" in favour of a steady stream of thuds.

"Catch you in the bathroom?" he asks, entering the apartment.

"No. Turning tomatoes," Nellie says, adjusting a tomato on her windowsill.

"How are you this week, Nellie?" He tilts his head like a puppy and looks, without blinking, into Nellie's eyes.

"Pregnant."

The minivan nurse takes a straight-backed chair from the kitchen and sets it in the living room. He opens his portfolio and sits down.

"We're going to show you a picture of two interlocking octagons and we want you to try to draw it."

"Who's 'we'? There's only one of you."

The minivan nurse points his pen at Nellie. "Very good. And there's only one of you."

"There's me and Aeolian."

"Who's Aeolian?" The minivan nurse smiles, motions for Nellie to sit down on the futon couch.

Nellie remains standing. "My fetus. It's just a nickname."

"Fine. The octagons." The minivan nurse smiles, lays a piece of paper on the coffee table. Motions again for Nellie to sit down.

"It means wind-borne. Did you know that?" Nellie asks, still standing.

"We're getting off track here." The minivan nurse pats the sheet of paper on the table.

"Thank goodness." Nellie crosses the room and

cranks her window open another few inches. She leans her head out the window, asks, "Do you like this heat?"

Dressed in a sleeveless, billowy frock and a pair of flip-flops, Nellie sits inside the bus shelter. She smooths her hands over the small floral print, stops to pick at the spots on her thighs where the cotton has balled up. When the bus appears at the end of the block Nellie steps out into the midmorning heat.

"You're late today," the driver says as Nellie steps into the bus.

"I'm just going in for coffee," Nellie says.

"You're gonna get fired for stuff like that."

"I can't get fired. I'm on disability."

No one asked me to doodle Leduc. I just happened to come across it, years before they moved their rigs into the area, one summer on my way up north to Peace River country for some tenting. I told a few rock-hounds that, for a reasonable fee, I'd give them the information that would change their futures. But they didn't bite. That crazy bunch would rather drill dusters based on "science" than pay me for a guaranteed gush-er. They drilled more than a 100 dry holes in a row before they happened on the Leduc reservoir. And I know why. Because the science of oil and gas exploration is like the science of childbirth. No matter how hard you study the oven, the proof is only in the pudding.

Unless you've got a uterus like mine.

The bus driver swings the door closed, glances back at Nellie. After putting the bus in gear, the driver turns to Nellie again.

"Is that your nightgown you're wearing?" the driver asks.

"Of course. Why would I wear somebody else's nightgown?" Nellie says as she spreads her knees wide and sinks into her seat.

The minivan nurse arrives carrying a plastic grocery store bag.

"Nellie, I've come before lunch today because we're going to make a tuna sandwich." The minivan nurse unpacks a can of tuna, a small jar of mayonnaise, and a loaf of brown bread.

"I only like the juice."

"What juice?"

"The tuna juice. The oil. The water. Whatever it's packed in." Nellie opens a drawer and pulls out a can opener.

"You drink that?" The minivan nurse watches Nellie work the opener around the top of the can.

"Straight."

"Nellie, you've worked in the food business for years. Nobody drinks tuna juice."

"It's whatever you're used to. When I'm off work I make my own menu." Nellie squeezes the lid into the tuna, drains the juice into her mouth.

Nellie walks to the end of her street, through a brown grassy area that Flo Mannville calls dog-shit park, until she comes to a chain-link fence. The fence separates the golf course from public property and extends down a steep incline to the centre of the riverbed. The Belly River is barely a trickle. Nellie picks her way down the slope, clutching the fence whenever her feet begin to slide out from under her. At the bottom she wobbles on a few large stones, trying to keep her feet out of the shallow creek, at the same time stooping to pick a margarine tub out from the creek bed. She shakes the water out of the tub. Still holding the margarine tub, Nellie makes her way around the end of the fence and up the steep incline to the golf course.

I remember the day of the Leduc

No. 1 ceremony because it was your mother's birthday. She was turning 15. She told me she found that box of Eddy matches on the road beside someone's Ford. I said, "Which Ford?" She said, "The red Tudor Sedan." Sure enough, there was one there. What could I do but believe her? Florence always had a good eye for cars.

Going up the incline is easier because Nellie can see the ground in front of her. Going downhill towards the creek, or down an escalator, or downstairs, Nellie's belly blocks the view. As she climbs, Nellie presses her hands into her thighs. Her heels slip off the ends of her flip-flops, so she backs her feet out completely, picks up the flip-flops and drops them into the margarine tub. By the time Nellie reaches level ground she can hear the tractors of the ground crew. Along the far side of the fairway, sprinklers spit water at regular intervals. Nellie strolls along the edge of the fairway in her bare feet, swinging her margarine tub.

"Barefoot on that grass? Are you fucking nuts?" Flo says over coffee at Doodlebugs. "I'm glad you're getting a hold of this thing and starting to exercise, but that grass could kill you."

"I can't find any shoes or sandals that don't bind my feet."

"I thought your feet were the same size as mine."

"Not anymore."

Flo peers under the table.

"They look small. Proportionately speaking. But puffy. What is that, edema? Why don't you show them to that nurse?"

"The minivan nurse? He doesn't like concrete stuff."

Flo Mannville sips her coffee. Sips again. Looks around Doodlebugs. "Are you wearing a nightgown?" she asks suddenly.

"A clean one. I'm not going to waste more money on maternity clothes."

"And the margarine tub?"

"You wouldn't believe how handy it is. None of that fishing around for sunglasses or a loonie, not knowing exactly what you have."

"The petrochemical purse. Not just for edible oils. Now, I wonder why the industry hasn't thought of that fashion starter?"

"They probably have. They make plastic shoes. Synthetic rubber raincoats. Polyester underwear."

"That minivan nurse," Flo speaks to the ceiling, "is more useless than a racked rig."

The minivan nurse arrives. He is flushed from knocking in the hot hallway. Nellie faces the window, flosses her teeth. The minivan nurse starts talking before he sits down.

"Nellie, today we're going to count backwards from 1000 in intervals of seven."

Nellie stops flossing, takes her hands away from her mouth to say, "I'm usually out walking by now. By the time we're done it's going to be a sauna out there."

"From 1000."

"It hardly cools down at all at night."

The minivan nurse closes his eyes, says slowly, "Nellie, I'm not here to talk weather. From 1000, please."

"I'm not talking weather. I'm talking climate." Nellie brings her hands back up to her mouth and begins to floss her molars.

Nellie creeps down the slope, balances around the end of the fence, and climbs up onto the golf course. At the edge of the fairway she picks a scorecard from the grass. She opens the card, reads the names and scores, and then follows the map. Each hole on the golf course has a name. Nellie walks tee to green through Sawtooth, Shunda, more slowly through Pekisko. By Nisku she is using the scorecard to stop sweat rivulets at her eyebrow. In the other hand she holds her margarine tub.

> Even though no one was smart enough to pay me for doodling Leduc, there was no sense letting

my gifted uterus go to waste. I knew the pool underlying the Leduc field was huge. So I tried a new tack for the next two wells, Leduc No. 2 and Atlantic No. 3.

"Hey fellas," I'd say to whoever was hanging around the No. 2 lease, "I wager this rig will hit a reef build-up of oil over 150 feet below Leduc No. 1."

"Bugger off," they'd say. Or worse.

"Quit hanging around here like a bad smell," I remember one rough-neck saying. He obviously didn't know anything about bad smells. He had whiskers. His gas mask wouldn't have sealed properly if they'd drilled into a pocket of hydrogen sulfide, like in Turner Valley. I'm not the type to say gas poisoning would have served him right.

I didn't pay any mind to the disre-spectful things those boys said, even when they called me Sour Gas Mary. Everybody who was anybody had a nickname.

"Who'll put a little cash on the table," I'd say, pulling my clutch out of my waistband. "Who'll wager that I'm wrong?" I'd open the clutch to show them that it was chock-a-block full of bills. Even though they'd roll their eyes and make the cuckoo sign with their fingers, they'd be in for ten or twenty.

Nellie turns as a twosome pulls their cart alongside her.

"No walking allowed," the woman driving says. She and her passenger wear brimmed hats and, on their noses, a thick layer of white zinc oxide.

Nellie stops, drops the scorecard into the margarine tub. She wraps her hand under her belly and feels the crescent of sweat between her underbelly and her crotch.

"The heat. Everyone has to take a cart. All the members voted for it," the passenger in the cart says.

"Are you a member?" the woman driving asks. "You should be wearing sun protection."

"Are you okay?" the passenger asks. "You look flushed."

"I'm pregnant," Nellie says.

"When I was pregnant I only gained eighteen pounds," the driver says.

"Don't let her make you feel bad," the passenger says. "I gained almost thirty-one-and-a-half pounds with my last baby. I was positively bovine."

"I'm not sure what I've gained. Around seventy kilograms, I guess."

"Good Lord," the driver says, "That sounds like a lot." The driver turns to her passenger. "Aren't kilograms bigger than pounds? I can never get that straight."

"Don't make her feel bad," the passenger says to the driver, and then turns to Nellie. "You should try Dr. Cost. She's great. Except in winter. She's a snowmobiler."

"She must have been disappointed with the mildness of last winter," the driver says. "There was no snow to speak of. And sleet at Christmas."

"I think I'll turn back here," Nellie says. "Is there a drinking fountain around?"

"Way back at Paskapoo," the passenger says.

"I'll look for a sprinkler," Nellie says.

"Epidural is the only way to go," the driver says before she steps on the pedal and steers the car towards the Nisku green.

"Oh no no no," the passenger calls over the jangle of the clubs in the back of the cart. "Water birth. Do a water birth. For your baby."

Nellie walks in the rough for shade. But the trees have been thinned and are too wide apart to provide a canopy. She breathes through a whistle-like hole in her lips, glances up at the black slice of sky that has just barely appeared in the west, accelerating towards her. Despite the advancing cloud, there is no relief from the heat. Nellie's nightgown is clingy, soaked with sweat. She looks up at the oily strip of sky above her, stumbles. The golf course is eerily silent. The hair on her arms rises. Nellie sees the course marshall, hunched, racing her cart down the other side of the fairway.

"Over here!" Nellie calls.

The marshal doesn't look or change directions and disappears over a rise in the fairway just before the sky explodes with a thunderous boom and an avalanche of golf-ball-sized hail.

"Fore!" Nellie screams, trying to cover her head with her margarine tub while running up the fairway for the shelter of the bigger trees. The ground shakes with another thunder clap. Golf balls drive down from the sky.

> When Leduc No. 2 took so long to hit paydirt, I revisited my clients. They were all depressed and doubled their wagers against me because they were sure that the well wasn't going to come in. They thought Leduc No. 1 was a freak. When No. 2 did come in, I pocketed a pretty sum. Just like doodling, I never had any trouble collecting. When a well blows in, everyone is loose with their cash. In all my days I was never stiffed by a rig worker who wasn't family.

Nellie lies on her back on the cool particleboard floor. Arms spread, legs spread, she still holds her margarine tub. Nellie is in the greenskeeper's shed. Beside her, under a work bench, is a plastic ice cream bucket. The lid of the bucket has several holes punched in it. Nellie pulls the bucket towards her, peels back the lid. Watches a clump of thin red worms wriggle away from the light into a sesame-seed bun.

Nellie can see the greenskeeper, the back of her T-shirt and ball cap, outside the shed. The greenskeeper talks to a teenage girl who sits on a tractor mower, puts her foot on the disc-shaped safety guard that covers the cutting blade.

"She's laid out on the floor," Nellie hears the greenskeeper say as she approaches the tractor, "right beside my new Winnipeg Red Wigglers."

"What happened to the old ones?"

"Died on me. Like the others. They all die as soon as I add any grass clippings."

"Maybe it's the fertilizer on the grass. I used to live near a petrochemical plant that made fertilizer. Whooee." The teenager fans the air in front her nose.

"I doubt it," the greenskeeper shrugs. "The other animals do all right here."

"The geese are out on Paskapoo again. One got brained with a golf ball."

"Good riddance to a nuisance."

"The rest are still there. Thinking they won't get hit."

"Hey," the greenskeeper lifts her chin in the direction of the gravel road leading up to the shed. "That must be the big gal's mother driving up now."

The teenager nods, "Nice truck."

"I would've expected her to be heavier," the greenskeeper says quietly as Florence Mannville steps down from the truck's cab, closes the door, adjusts the bridge of her glasses.

"It's usually a willpower thing, not genetic," the teenager reaches for the key in the tractor's ignition.

"That is a nice truck," the greenskeeper says as Florence approaches.

Nellie peels the lid off the bucket again. She puts her hand in and plucks out a handful of worms, plops them into her margarine tub.

> As a doodlebugger, I'd get a flat rate when the rig hit paydirt. So doodlebugging was easy: set my fee, maybe do a little witch show, point to the spot, sit back while the hole was drilled, collect my money. Mind you, they took a lot longer to drill in those days, especially when they were still using cable rigs. Still, there was only one transaction for each well. Easy as rhubarb pie. But to make money in Leduc I had to enter into a transaction with almost everyone. And every time I had to size up my client, plan an approach, start up a conversation, ignore a few insults, record all my clients on foolscap so I could collect afterwards. It was work. Hard nonstop work. If I

wanted to work that hard I would
have been a stenographer.

Flo cranks the air conditioning in her truck to full as she drives Nellie through the winding golf course road, away from the greenskeeper's shed.

"Nice to have a little breeze," Nellie says, flapping her arms so the air can circulate in her armpits. "When did you get the truck?"

Flo ignores a reduced-speed sign and a depiction of crossing golfers.

"When you drill a well," Flo says, "you want to take the most direct route. Straight down. But sometimes you can't, and you gotta do a little whipstocking. So you send your whipstock down the line and redirect the bit. But once you start whipstocking you've got yourself some more problems. More scrapings, more round trips, key-seats, doglegs, shoulders, the lot. And sometimes, you gotta ask, 'is this worth it?'"

Nellie points to the right, to a tee box, where a golfer lines a club up to a ball. "I think she's about to hit across the road here."

Flo steps on the gas, jabs her middle finger toward the golfer.

"I must have a whipstocking uterus," Nellie says as they speed in front of the golfer.

"Whatever," Flo grumbles. "Your bit's been walking on its own and it's time for a realignment."

After Leduc No. 2, the next Leduc

well was Atlantic No. 3 in the spring of 1948. Whoosh. Kaboom. The well went wild and vomitted oil for 6 months and 40 acres. 40 acres of simmering, bubbling blackstrap molasses. And the smell. Lordy, the smell.

They stopped Atlantic No. 3 by whipstocking two relief wells, one from the south and one from the west, which intersected with the Atlantic hole. They blew water, cement, feathers, sawdust, and even cotton-seed hulls down the relief holes. Eventually they plugged the wild well with suppositories made of gunny sacks rolled up in chicken wire. I was 53 years old. More than 30 years experience under my straw hat. But nobody thought to ask me. Sanitary napkins would have plugged that well from the start.

Flo parks in front of Nellie's apartment. She hops out of the driver's side and walks around to help Nellie. Nellie's door swings open. A thick bare foot dangles.

"You're close," Flo says.

Nellie's foot drops a little further.

"Almost," Flo says.

Nellie's toes settle on the running board.

"There. Thanks. It would be so much easier if I could see that first step." Nellie closes the truck door.

"What do you think of it?" Flo puts her hands on her hips.

"Of what?"

"The truck. Do you like it? Extra-long box, no trunk."

Nellie walks around the truck, peers in a window, returns to Flo's side.

"Good concept, Mom. But you're still in a closed-minded trunk when it comes to my pregnancy."

"Me and everyone else. Doesn't that tell you something?"

"Must be getting cramped in there."

"Maybe I'll try another approach. Drill in from a different direction."

"You're aiming for the same reservoir. Disbelief."

"Given the facts, what else would I aim for?"

"The alternative." Nellie nudges her belly into Flo's side. "Instead of drilling in, drill out."

"The heat's getting to you again," Flo points at Nellie's apartment building. "Do you have any beers?"

"In my fridge."

"I can only stay for a bunch," Flo says as they walk up the sidewalk.

"At least you're keeping busy," Flo Mannville says one Saturday morning.

"It's a cooler colour, I think," Nellie says.

"You gonna paint the whole apartment black?"

"Yep."

Flo Mannville unwraps the cellophane from a new pack of cigarettes. She opens the cupboard under the sink to put the cellophane in the garbage.

"What've you got here?" Flo drags a plastic crate out from under the sink. Nellie dips the roller into the black paint, runs it up and down the slope of the paint tray. Flo pulls the lid off the crate.

"What've you got this bin of moldy tomatoes and shredded paper under here for?" Flo pulls a tangled clump out of the crate, examines it in her hand, continues, "And dirt. There's dirt in here, too." She jerks her hand away from her face, shakes her hand above the bin. "For chrissakes, its full of worms. Did you know that?"

"That's not dirt," Nellie says as she rolls a black "W" on the wall, then fills it in with horizontal strokes. "Those are worm castings."

"Shit?" Flo wipes her palms on each other.

"That's right." Nellie bends to dip the roller again.

The minivan nurse arrives.

"Nellie, if you had a loonie, and then you bought a stamp for your letter, how much change would you have left?"

"I don't write letters. I'm too busy receiving e-mail from my dead grandmother."

"How much change, Nellie?"

"There's an e-mail waiting for me now."

"Because you don't want to answer the question?"

"No, because the lights have gone on in the bathroom."

For a while, Nellie flings worm castings out her ground-level window, covering Flo's old cigarette butts and the brown patch of lawn. When the lawn is sufficiently coated, Nellie begins to collect the excess castings in margarine containers. She prints labels:

turbo castings

"There is no best-before date," Nellie explains to the minivan nurse when she places a labeled margarine tub in his lap. "The castings will keep forever in the plastic containers."

"The thing is," Flo says over subsidized coffee in Doodlebugs, "I'm reaching the end of my drill stem on this matter."

"I'm going to get some more." Nellie points at the little house she has made of ketchup packets. She walks to the condiment counter and grabs a handful of relish packets. Flo drums her fingers on her coffee cup while she waits for Nellie.

In October, when everyone was calming down, Atlantic No. 3 caught fire. The day before Labour Day a little hill formed under the derrick and the derrick started to shimmy. Over the day the hill rose like a blister until it touched the bottom of the doghouse and the derrick started to teeter and totter. That night the whole rig fell over. Left nothing but a crater with the kelly and the swivel sticking out. Around two in the morning a globe of fire rose up from the centre of the crater, floated for a second, and then rocketed into the sky. Spontaneous combustion. That fire burned for three days.

Your mother and I camped on the corner of the Atlantic No. 3 lease. We said we were with the Morning Albertan. Florence was 16. She got a job right away, driving a plow, building up the fire barriers. She washed the grease off herself with gasoline. Earned enough money

from Atlantic No. 3 to buy a Chevy
Coupe from one of the fellas. And
she started smoking in front of me.
16 years old. Working her mouth
like a goldfish, blowing perfect
smoke rings like Leduc No.1.

"Relish," Nellie says when she returns. "For the lawn.
And creamer for the chimney." She lays the packets
around the ketchup house. Stacks the creamer containers.
"How's this for nesting?"

"How can you be so oblivious, Nellie. Do we have to
go through another two years? When is it going to end?"

"Not today."

"Start today. Get back in range."

"Driving range?" Nellie asks as she straightens the
creamers.

"You know what kind of range I mean. And you have
moved beyond it."

Nellie flattens the ketchup house with one hand,
scoops all the packets into her margarine container.

"Your truck has a long box. Where do you find room
to park it downtown?" Nellie asks.

Florence glances towards Sauerkraut, who is walking
across the cafeteria. "I'm consulting from home," Flo says.

"Fired?"

Flo pauses before she replies, "Retired."

"Guess you're not in the driving range either." Nellie
raises her coffee cup. "Cheers."

Sauerkraut's slim skirt sparkles in the cafeteria light.

"The truck?" Nellie asks.

"I needed something to haul all my stuff home from the office. I had a lot of stuff. Two truckloads. And I left the desk."

"Good morning, ladies," Sauerkraut calls to them. "I'd stop to chat but I haven't time again. We're always short-staffed. How's the Imp running, Nellie?"

"Of course you're short-staffed," Flo snaps back. "You need Nellie." Then Flo says to Nellie, "We should stay here for lunch. Put a Band-Aid in our burritos."

"Fur-eatos. Why would we do that?"

"So we could get our lunch free. Haven't you heard of that old trick?"

Here's the thing about Atlantic No. 3 I always leave out: that Coupe that your mother bought, that first car, well, doesn't the fella that used to own it come by my house in Calgary one night. That house on the north hill. You'd remember the backyard. I built you a treehouse. Not that you ever went up. Scared of heights. Anyway, one night before your mother met Jim Brody, this cleaned-up rigger comes to the door. Just off the rig. New jeans. New haircut. Cheeks shinier than the courthouse banister. Your mother was away, driving a water truck in Dunvegan.

This fella at my door claims your mother never paid him for the car. The Coupe. I told him to chase himself around the block.

In the end, I had to pay that buffed-up rig-boy $500. The going rate for a used Chevy Coupe. Or so he said. Anything to get his shiny face off my property. When your mom came home for her 7 days out I put it to her. "Florence Mannville, did you steal that Coupe from a Leduc rig-boy?" She said, "I only take what's rightfully mine." She said the same thing when I discovered my steel-toed boots missing. Ned gave me those boots. We had the same size feet. Same size as your mother.

VI

Flo stands in the shallow end of the swimming pool. The top half of her slick black bathing suit is dry. She skims her arms over the surface of the water. Nellie floats, face down, beside her. The back of Nellie's bra is raised above the surface, as is the white cotton seat of her underpants.

"Don't you think people will notice you're not wearing a bathing suit?" Flo asks when Nellie rolls over, revealing the grey-white cups of her bra.

"They won't say anything," Nellie says.

"To your face," Flo scoffs.

"I'm not going to buy a maternity bathing suit, and there's no way I'd fit into my old one-piece. A two-piece was the practical alternative. Even if the pieces are a bit snug."

"You have no shame, Nellie."

"That's right." Nellie rolls over and puts her face back in the water.

You were just a baby in 1959 when

Florence decided to go to Swan Hills. She insisted on getting a trailer like the other lease families. Florence was only 26 years old but somehow she acquired a 32 footer. It was twice as big as some of the other trailers. Brand new, too. I don't know how she managed. Be darned if I was going to contribute cash to a scheme that had me playing nanny in Swan Hills. Still, I would have opened my wallet had I known that the trailer was built in California. We should have paid to have it insulated. A canvas tent would have been warmer than that tin contraption.

We kept the little oil heater going all the time in the trailer. Except . . . when the weather turned colder the heater would stop. So I'd be out in the middle of the night, standing on the boards I'd set around the trailer so I wouldn't sink into the daytime mud, thawing the lines from the oil barrel with a little flame. There'd be other women out around the other trailers. The wives of the rig crew. But I

wasn't a wife. I was a doodlebugger.
My innate ability was being wasted.
I don't think Florence appreciated
that. She never acknowledged my
innate ability. Or the waste.

Nellie treads water, tips backwards, lets her toes rise to the surface. "Do you suppose this is what a bird feels like?"

"It's hard to imagine you riding an air current." Flo points to the men's locker room. "Hey, here comes the assistant. I met him when I registered us. He does all the paperwork."

A grey-haired man, sliding his aluminum cane ahead of him, shuffles across the pool deck. He wears red swim trunks pulled up high on his naval. He has long bony limbs. Grey wisps sprout from his chest and armpits. He settles into a deck chair at the edge of the pool.

"He looks familiar," Nellie says. "That weird-shaped cane is like the one embedded in the Imp."

"He's a crabby old fuck," Flo says. "I filled out the forms in black ink and he wanted me to re-do them in blue. He was swinging that cane around like a tire iron."

A small elderly woman comes out from the women's change room. She wears a fuchsia maillot, strides across the pool area to the man in the chair. She hands the man her towel, then proceeds toward Flo and Nellie. At the edge of the pool, she adjusts the neoprene weights strapped around her papery wrists and ankles.

"That's the instructor," Flo says. "She must be 150 years old. A regular fossil."

"She looks familiar too. Is this a seniors' class?" Nellie asks Flo.

"I didn't want to start you on anything too extreme. Remember what happened when you exerted yourself at the golf course?"

"Wasn't there a prenatal class?"

"It didn't occur to me to check."

A few senior citizens, mostly women, straggle into the pool. The speakers whistle, then emit the first twangs of Babs Howard's "Roughstock."

"This should be all right," Flo says. "Good music."

"Ten-minute warm-up," the tiny instructor orders as she slides into the pool. The woman gestures to the man in the chair. "John here will point out any slackers."

Flo laughs.

"Or laughers. Recumbent cycling now. Lie back, slow jog, knees to surface. Two three four," the instructor calls.

Nellie lies back. Her knees rhythmically break the surface of the water.

Florence hitched the trailer to her car; she was driving a Pontiac then. You and I stayed in the trailer, close to your diapers and food and crib. The crib was a masterpiece. I made it with wood scraps and sanded it until it felt smooth as bathwater. When you didn't need it, the sides folded flat and the entire unit snapped onto the wall.

"How are you doing that?" Flo sputters at Nellie. "I can't cycle without sinking."

"Just think about something else." Nellie calmly cycles, her face pointed towards the ceiling.

Flo's face disappears under the water, reappears when she stands up, coughing.

The man in the chair points his cane at Florence.

"Recumbent cycling or out," the instructor shouts at Flo.

The summer had been rainy, but even the excess rain couldn't account for the soupy condition of the road leading in to Swan Hills. It was the muskeg creeping up.

The Pontiac started slipping and spinning in the mud, and so did the trailer. Every so often Flo would get out and clean the mud from under the fender wells. We passed a few abandoned vehicles. Older cars that no one had bothered to retrieve after they got stuck. When we passed a water truck that had been abandoned, I knew we were done for. Ahead there was a slight dip in the road and then a long incline, a couple of miles to the top of the rise. There were cars stuck helter-

skelter all over the lower part of the
hill.

The instructor distributes two batons to everyone in the class. At each end of the batons are plastic flotation doughnuts.

"Everyone have your flotation? On to abs. V-sit. Toes up and crunch."

Nellie's toes point to the ceiling. Her hands, gripping the flotation sticks, stretch out at right angles to her body.

"Lovely, graceful," the instructor says to Nellie.

Beside Nellie, Flo lays back, kicks. The instructor approaches her.

"There's no need to kick," the instructor says. "You have flotation. We're working our abdominals, not our legs."

Flo stretches out her arms, raises one foot out of the water, raises the other foot for a moment. Then sinks.

"Do you think this is the right class for you?" the instructor asks.

"I'm a senior. I'm sixty-seven years old. This is a senior's class."

"Just jog on the spot for this section. There's a prenatal class if you're looking for something gentler."

Flo stepped on the gas. We jerked through the dip and started fish-tailing up the rise. I laid some blankets on the floor where I sat with you on my lap and tried to keep our balance. I'm sure Florence, if she could take one hand off the steering wheel, was waving at all the people in the stuck vehicles.

We got as far as a pipe truck that was nearly broadside on the road. Florence tried to scoot by on the inside, and she almost made it, but we slid sideways into the pipe truck's tracks. We were so close that the Pontiac's bumper was almost touching the pipe truck's rear mud flaps. There was about a half-dozen cars stuck in front of the pipe truck and about 20 cars behind us.

"Arms only, now. Slide your flotation devices behind your knees and hold them there by bending your legs. That's it, what's your name? Nellie. Now swing the arms from side to side. Like Nellie."

"I have no idea what she's talking about," Flo says.

"It's just like driving," Nellie says.

"It's nothing like driving. When I drive I'm in control."

"Just pretend the flotation is the seat and that you're steering through an S-turn."

"Where's the gas pedal? Where's the steering wheel? Where's the ashtray?"

"Nellie," the instructor calls, "could you ask the woman beside you to pay attention."

A cat was towing the cars in front of us, one by one, up the rest of the grade and over the rise. We waited in the trailer for about 6 hours. Flo came back for a while to visit and we all ate a bit of jarred baby food since everything else was boxed up. Prunes, I think. A jar of pureed prunes.

The mud on the road came over the top of Florence's gum boots. I'd been around a lot of mud in my life. Sometimes it smelled like good old potting soil. In Turner Valley and Leduc the mud smelled like sulpher. But in Swan Hills that blue-black mud smelled like shower mold. And it stuck like plaster. I bet Flo's boots weighed 20 pounds each. A little baby like you could have drowned in that mud.

When it was the pipe truck's turn to be towed, the catskinner signalled for Florence to come and talk to him. Florence waded through the mud because she knew catskinners never got out of their cat. The catskinner told Florence that this was his last trip. That he was towing the pipe truck over the rise and then calling it a day.

Florence was mad. I could tell by the way she kept pushing her glasses up the bridge of her nose. When the catskinner rolled away to hook up the pipe truck, Florence went to her Pontiac's trunk and pulled out the tire chains she had packed for winter driving. She used the chains to fasten her car to the pipe truck. So when the cat started pulling the pipe truck, we were dragged along behind. Flo in the driver's seat of the car and you and I slipping about in the trailer. At the top, Flo had to use a snow shovel to get the mud off her windshield. Those mud flaps on the pipe truck didn't help one bit.

The man points the rubber tip of his cane at Flo.

"I'm going to have to ask you leave," the instructor says. "You're a distraction."

"What did I do?" Flo asks.

"You're not in sync with the music. Or with the rest of the class."

"My whole body is under water. How can that be distracting?"

"In this class we are concerned about the subsurface. We know what you are doing and what you are not doing."

"Can you see what I'm doing with my middle finger?"

Florence told me afterwards that hooking us to the pipe truck maybe wasn't such a good idea. Especially with the tire chains. Especially with the steep riverbank to the side. She said if the chain had broken the car brakes wouldn't have been enough to keep us on the road. She said it all as though I couldn't have thought of those drawbacks myself.

"You didn't have to get out with me," Flo says to Nellie. They stand naked under side-by-side shower heads.

"I'd had enough anyway. I was getting thirsty." Nellie opens her mouth under the shower, gulps until the shower shuts off. Flo's shower turns off at the same time.

"What's with these things?" Flo asks as she punches the button on the wall and the shower starts again.

"Maybe they don't want to waste water," Nellie says, walking across the shower area to get her towel.

"That's going a bit overboard," Flo says. "I need a good long pounding shower. I can feel my muscles stiffening up already from that aqua boot camp. I should have gotten kicked out earlier."

Swan Hills was Florence's first go at roughnecking. She'd been working on the rigs since she was 16, driving fire plow, tank truck, and water truck, but she'd never worked on the drill table. In Swan Hills there was a toolpush who said he'd let a woman on his crew. That's why we went up there.

Flo didn't mind 12-hour shifts. She learned the work right away. She wasn't some kid just out of the hayfield. Not that those kids didn't turn out to be good workers. But Florence knew things from the start.

Near the end of her last shift before her first long change, or week off, the driller asked Florence to get a core sample that had been lying around the doghouse. As a roughneck, Florence took orders from the driller so she went into the office and picked up the core sample, even though she couldn't imagine why he needed it. She stuck the core in the big side pocket of her coveralls so her hands would be free in case the driller called at her for something else. As she walked out of the doghouse she saw, just for a few seconds, the rest of the crew standing in a group in front of her. "Congratulations," the driller said, "you're in." Then he took Flo's hard hat off her head, turned the hat upside down, raised it in the air, and cracked it down on my Florence's head.

Florence was ecstatic. When she came to the trailer that night she couldn't stop talking about being walloped on the head. How she just saw a flash of white. How she didn't think she could keep standing, but she did. How it was like being sober, drunk, and then sober again. All in a minute. She used a term that I suppose doesn't shock anyone these days. She said she had been turtle-fucked. She was proud of being turtle-fucked.

Nellie dries under her armpits, under her breasts, and drags the towel through her crotch. Then she drapes her towel around her shoulders and, squatting slightly, straddles the shower-room drain.

"Are you doing what I think you're doing?" Flo asks from under her shower. She wipes water from her eyes.

"Peeing," Nellie says.

"The toilet's only twenty feet away," Flo points.

"The stalls are small and I'm not. This is easier." Nellie jiggles the lower half of her body, stands up.

"And I'm the one who gets kicked out of aquasize," Flo calls after Nellie.

Flo kept the core sample. She pulled it out of her coveralls when she came into the trailer and rolled it across the floor to you. That core sample ended up being one of your favourite playthings. Later, she had it cut in half to make bookends.

Flo lies on a bench in the change room. She has a towel wrapped around her body and her hands crossed over her chest. Her eyes are closed.

"That was brutal. I feel like I've been turtle-fucked," Flo says.

"Maybe water isn't your medium," Nellie suggests as she pulls open her locker door. "You'll get better with practice." Nellie takes her towel from her shoulders and drops it on the floor.

Flo rolls her head to one side. "I have no intention of coming here again."

"It was your idea to come and get some exercise. You said it would be good for both of us. You did say 'both of us'."

While Nellie untangles her thong underwear and Flo continues to lie on the bench, a naked woman with a towel wrapped around her head enters their locker room nook. The woman is about Flo's size and age. She is humming. Flo raises her eyebrows, nudges Nellie. Nellie turns.

"Hello," the woman says as she works the combination lock on a locker.

"Aren't you Babs Howard?" Flo asks.

"Yes. That's me."

"Babs Howard the country singer?"

"The same."

"I knew it. I could tell by the fringe on your towel. I'm Florence Mannville and this is my daughter Nellie."

"Pleased to meet you," Nellie says, hauling a bucket of petroleum jelly out of her locker, peeling off the lid, and scooping out some of the jelly with her fingers. She massages the jelly into her nipples.

"Sore nipples," Flo says quickly, and laughs nervously as she slides Nellie's bucket under the bench with her foot.

"Big nipples," Babs says.

"It's just a stage or something," Flo says.

"Magnificent nipples," Babs says.

Nellie licks the petroleum jelly from her fingers. Florence looks at the ceiling.

"If you're hungry," Babs says, "I've got some cookies

here. I'm going to an Oil Wives luncheon today." She pulls a narrow tray out of her locker, removes the cellophane from the top, and passes the cookies to Nellie and Flo. "Date pinwheels," Babs says. "Worth the effort, don't you think?"

Nellie takes a handful of the spiral shaped cookies.

"No thanks," Flo says, without looking in the container.

Florence got a migraine that night, after being cracked on the head. Around midnight she moved from the top bunk to the floor. Her headache was so bad that she crawled to your diaper bucket to throw up. When she went to the rig the next morning her eyes were red as a sunburned neck. I'd never seen her look so rough.

Babs sets the cookie tray on the bench before she unwinds the towel from her head, lets her wet hair fall down her back. She shakes a bottle of hair mousse, squirts some into her hand, and works it through her hair.

"Been swimming?" Nellie asks.

"Riding. The stationary bike upstairs."

Flo stands up, says, "I thought you'd be riding horses out on the range. Wild horses. Broncs."

"The only things I ride are the stationary cycle upstairs and my husband at home."

Babs takes her hand-held hair dryer to an electrical outlet around the corner. Nellie and Flo hear the tinny whir of the dryer on high speed.

> I let Florence talk me into Swan Hills because I thought I'd be able to doodle the south hills. There were several oil companies working the area and I figured at least one of them might want to tighten their drilling prospects. I had no idea I'd be muckbound in a trailer. I was glad to get back to my house on Calgary's north hill. I needed a base camp that wasn't a prison. Not that I didn't enjoy my special time with you.

"Pinwheel cookies. Husband. Mousse. Babs is a fraud," Flo says.

"So what?" Nellie pulls her muumuu over her head. "The pinwheels are still good. She can still yodel."

"I feel manipulated."

"It's her job to manipulate. She's an entertainer."

"She's supposed to be a frontier woman. I've been duped." Flo opens her locker with a bang.

"Get a hold of yourself, Mom. Whipstock her."

"How's that?"

"Whipstock. Use the part of Babs' casing that's workable. As for the rest, mill a window and whipstock out to a better reservoir."

"What do you know about whipstocks?" Flo reaches into her locker for her bra.

"Everything you told me."

"Well," Flo shakes her bra at Nellie, "you've got to use a gyro tool before you whipstock. You need one to orient yourself first to make sure you're going in the right direction."

"This pregnancy is my orientation. "

Flo looks down at the bench for a few moments.

"Do you think this tray of cookies will fit in my gym bag?" Flo asks.

"The Oil Wives may never forgive you," Nellie says.

VII

Flo stands on her front lawn beside a huge brown fir tree. In one hand she holds a chainsaw, in the other she holds a red canister. Signalling with the blade of the saw, she directs Nellie to park the Imp in the driveway, near the house, rather than at the curb.

"I need you to park on the driveway. I'm gonna drop this big boy onto the street," Flo says, pointing the chainsaw at the dead fir. "Don't want to hit the Imp." Flo sets the chainsaw on the lawn and removes the cap on the spout of the gas canister. "Then I'll hook it to my truck and tow it to one side, off the road."

Nellie swings open the Imp's door. Pushes her hands into the seat to help lift her weight out of the vehicle. "Why today? It's Christmas."

"New chainsaw. Christmas present to myself. Check it out." Flo turns the chainsaw so Nellie can see all sides. "Two-stroke engine. Gas and oil. Besides, if I don't bring this tree down, it's liable to fall towards the house next time we have one of those weird storms."

"Doesn't look like sleet this year," Nellie leans against the Imp, pats the convertible's soft top. "But I put the top up just in case."

"I'm glad you're up for the diner this year," Flo says as she fills the chainsaw's tank. "I missed the tradition last Christmas."

"What killed the tree?"

"Lack of water. Strange weather. Or its time had come. It's as old as the house. Stand at the end of the driveway there and let me know if anyone's coming down the street. Wave your arms or something." Flo pulls the starter cord. The motor sputters.

"Don't you need safety goggles?" Nellie asks.

"I'm already wearing them." Flo taps the arm of her regular glasses, winks. She pulls the cord again, adjusts the choke as the motor revs. The air fills with the smell of gas. Using a downward motion, Flo zips off a few of the lower branches so she can get closer to the trunk. Moving in to the trunk, she cuts a wedge from the street-side of the tree. Stepping around to work on the opposite side, the house-side of the tree, Flo makes a slice into the trunk. She pulls the saw out, pauses. Flo looks up. She tries to topple the tree by pushing on the trunk, above the cut, with one hand. The tree doesn't budge so Flo works the saw into the trunk again, slicing deeper.

"Mom!" Nellie calls.

Flo concentrates on the cut she is making.

"Fore!" Nellie calls.

Flo looks up, tries to yank her saw out of the tree trunk. She looks up again, quickly, and lets go of the saw.

Flo ducks and scurries from the oncoming branches. The top of the tree hits the house with a crackle of branches followed by a thud of the trunk. The tree slides sideways, screeching along the eaves towards the driveway. When only the top branches are touching the eaves, the tree drops across the driveway, sinks into the Imp's roof.

Flo and Nellie stand in their places until Flo moves forward and picks up the buzzing chainsaw from beside the ragged stump. Flo switches the saw off, exhales.

"I have no idea how that happened. Not a fucking clue. Must've been leaning this way before I started cutting. But it didn't look like it."

They approach the Imp, survey the cratered top, the shattered side windows, the bulging doors.

"I don't use the top much anyway," Nellie says, wiping brown needles off the bumper.

"We'll never get anyone to haul that tree off today. And I can't get the truck out of the garage with the Imp here. Nice friggin' way to spend Christmas."

"Let's look at the alternatives. What's in your fridge?"

"Beer."

"Any tomato juice?"

"Probably in the cupboard. Probably expired. I used to drink Bloody Marys when your grandma was alive."

"We'll mix up a few Red Eyes."

"I could use one. Amazing I didn't kill one of us. Fucking miracle."

"'Tis the season," Nellie says, leading her mother into the house.

Nellie's water cooler glugs as Sauerkraut fills a mug with water. She wears a long black sundress with spaghetti straps. Her white shoulder blades protrude like dorsal fins.

"Oh Nellie, I've been meaning to stop by. But you know, after the last round of layoffs I've been run off my espadrilles. Tell me everything you've been doing. Absolutely everything."

"You see me at the cafeteria almost every day. I'm there for coffee," Nellie says from her beanbag chair.

Holding the mug in both hands, Sauerkraut settles onto the couch. She crosses her legs, looks around at Nellie's black walls.

"I like the colour. How's your mother?"

"You see her almost every day, too."

Nellie reaches her arm over the side, picks a clear hose up from the floor. The hose, attached to the water tank, has a bull clip at the end. Nellie unclips the hose, inserts the end into her mouth.

"Sometimes friends just need to drop in to get the whole story." Sauerkraut looks again at the walls, clears her throat. "How's the Imperial?"

"My water pipeline," Nellie gulps, re-clips the hose, waves it in the air.

"Still running?" Sauerkraut asks.

"Never need to wash out my glass," Nellie says.

"Are you able to drive these days?" Sauerkraut asks,

untying her sandal and sliding out her long foot. She polishes her toenail with her thumb. "Can you believe the heat? Imagine. Open-toed shoes in January. It must be very uncomfortable for you in that car. Getting in and out. Especially in this heat."

Nellie leans closer. Distinguishes a tiny saguaro cactus on Sauerkraut's big toenail. Each of the other toenails hosts an orange and yellow sunset.

"I'm ready to come back to work," Nellie says. Sauerkraut's mouth opens. She looks directly at Nellie. "Is that what your doctor said?"

"No."

"Well then. Let's talk about the record-breaking heat. Or your Imperial. Thinking of selling?"

> I've discovered a recipe for preventing stretch marks. Hope it's not too late! Hah hah hah.
>
> > 1/2 cup extra-virgin olive oil
> > 1/4 cup aloe vera gel
> > 6 capsules vitamin E, cut open
> > 4 capsules vitamin A, cut open
>
> Mix ingredients in a blender. Once a day, apply the oil externally to the abdomen, hips, and thighs. Refrigerate excess.
>
> Excess? Well, they didn't have you in mind.

"That was a lovely visit," Sauerkraut says as she reaches for the door handle. "You'll have to drive over, in the Imp of course, and see my place some time."

"When?" Nellie hands Sauerkraut a sour cream container of worm castings.

Sauerkraut looks at the label on the lid.

"When should I come over?" Nellie asks.

"Mmm?" Sauerkraut checks that the lid is tightly sealed on the container.

"To your place."

Sauerkraut has one hand on the doorknob. With the other hand she brings the container to her nose, sniffs. Sniffs again. She smiles slightly, answers "Mother's Day."

"Mother's Day it is then." Nellie points to the container. "That shouldn't smell."

"Won't you be busy with your mother?"

"She'll come along."

You're lucky you don't have hemorrhoids. You'd have to be a contortionist for some of these Internet remedies.

"Hemorrhoids: apply cold witch hazel compresses to the affected area. Keep feet and legs elevated while eliminating."

Walk a mile a day. Now that makes

sense. No gymnastics required. No
excess to refrigerate.

After Sauerkraut leaves, Nellie lies down on her bed.
She counts the tomatoes around her room. Rolls from her
side to her back. Takes a red tomato off her headboard and
bites. Chews. Climbs out of bed, goes to the bathroom,
pees, grabs a red pencil from the kitchen drawer, and
returns to the bedroom. On her black bedroom wall
Nellie creates a chart.

HOME BIRTH

PROS	CONS
- gazpacho	- room too small
- parking for Imp	- possibility of minivan nurse
- doodlebug/computer	- lack of service
	- only one set of bedding
	- squashed tomatoes

HOSPITAL BIRTH

PROS	CONS
- free pads	- not sick
- free stool softeners	- room too bright
- free spray bottle for perineum	- possibility of minivan nurse
	- possibility of doctor
	- possibility of enema

After her afternoon nap, Nellie makes an addition to
the chart:

OTHER: consider Imp, cafeteria, greenhouse, pool, etc.

Flo plops a gym bag on the table in Doodlebugs. Nellie steadies her coffee.

"There you go," Flo says. The bag has her old company logo stitched on the outside. She reaches into the bag and pulls out a stack of blue coveralls, similar to the ones Nellie wore on the rig tour, but smaller. They all have Flo's old company logo stitched on the breast pocket.

"Those aren't going to fit me," Nellie says.

"They're not for you. They're for the baby. Size small."

Nellie props herself into a standing position, takes the coveralls from Flo. Flo sits down. Nellie holds the coveralls up by the shoulders. Peers down to where the bottoms of the overall touch her shins.

"You don't believe I'm carrying a baby."

"You can use the gym bag as a diaper bag." Flo lights a cigarette, streams smoke at the ceiling.

"But you don't believe I'm going to have a baby."

"An opportunity arose. What am I going to do with all these overalls?"

"What kind of opportunity? I thought the company retired you."

"Let's just say I happened to be in the vicinity of the stockroom."

Nellie folds the coveralls into thirds, sets them on the table.

"I'm going to get a bunch of those pats of butter to have with my coffee. Do you want some? They're free."

I always had trouble talking to your
mother. She talked back. Barked

back. When your mother was little I'd ask, "Florence, would you like porridge this morning?" and she'd say, even when she was very small, "I'd rather suck a fart from a bull."

So different from you. When I would ask, "Nellie, would you like porridge for breakfast this morning?" you'd ask back, "Is there any pork roast left?" Sometimes I thought you weren't listening. But then I realized you heard every word.

Of course, you both got porridge.

The bottom of the door bounces slightly into Nellie's apartment. A kick. Nellie opens the door and notices, first, the shoes. Shrivelled snakeskin pumps.

"Hello Bitty."

"I'm going by 'Bit.'"

"What happened to the greenhouse?" Nellie asks, stepping aside so Bit, who balances a full jug of water on each shoulder, can enter the apartment.

"Too much oxygen. I was worried the Firefly might spontaneously combust."

Bit enters Nellie's apartment and walks toward the cooler stand. She sets one of the jugs on the stand, the other on the floor.

For a while there was an emergency drill at your mother's school where they showed the kids how to protect themselves from atomic fallout by hiding under a picnic blanket. The principal came from America where fallout shelters were all the rage. Our Prime Minister had a shelter, but he was about the only person in Canada who bothered. Every time Florence was under her picnic blanket she gouged holes in the floor with her pen. She said she was digging for treasure. She wasn't a little kid, she was a teenager. You should have seen the size of the holes by the time I was called in. I believe she would have found some treasure had it not been for the cement underlay.

Once I saw an ad in an American magazine for a wide-brimmed hat that was supposed to protect you from the heat flash of an atomic bomb. What sort of ninny would believe such a thing? Imagine, there I'd be, standing on the platform expecting the drill to bite into a pocket of pressurized natural gas, sparks, friction, emergency flares, on my tiptoes in case of a blowout, there weren't always blowout-pre-venters then, and there I'd be wear-ing a floppy atomic bomb hat. I don't think so. The lighter the better if you have to run. I've heard of blokes out-running blowouts. Don't suppose anyone could outrun atomic fallout.

"Have you checked your mail today?" Bit asks as she reaches into the pocket of her suit jacket and pulls out her invoice book.

"I check whenever the lights flicker in the bathroom."

"So you got the note from the manager?"

"I thought you meant e-mail. I haven't opened my mailbox in the hall for months."

"What if there's a reminder for your car tune-up in there?"

"My mother reminds me of stuff like that."

"Well, you should check your mail today. The note from the manager says we're gonna have to buy our apart-ments or get out." Bit tears the water invoice out of her book and hands it to Nellie. "Condominiumizing."

"You want to buy a condominium? Only a nutbar would buy a block of air," Flo Mannville says. "I'll help you buy something tangible. Like land. Like a new car."

"I've got a car. I just need a bit more cash."

"The Imp's not a car. It's a float."

"Your house is a block of air."

"It's the lot that counts. There's no point buying real estate unless you get some earth. Even your worms know that."

"They make their own soil. They need air."

"You need something you can dig into."

"I'll dig worm castings."

"Try the bank," Flo says, stubbing her cigarette on the outside windowsill.

Nellie presses her palms together, touches her index fingers to her lips. After a moment she says, "Air circulates carbon."

"The bank," Flo says as she locks the window latch. "Air is free. I'm not loaning you money to buy something that's free."

The minivan nurse hands Nellie an unlined sheet of paper and a pencil.

"Today, Nellie, I'd like it if we could draw a house."

"I won't need the pencil."

"Would you prefer a crayon?"

"I'll just trace with my finger. It's an airy house with a wind farm out back."

Nellie fashions a large, conical sunhat out of newspaper

and duct tape. She pulls on her largest muumuu. Sitting spread-legged on the couch, huffing, she reaches for a felt-tipped pen, draws sandal straps on the top of her bloated feet. Nellie pops on her conical hat, her sunglasses, and steps outside her apartment into the daylight. She stands at the front door for a minute, considering the glare of the sun. She returns to her apartment and tears the ends off a cracker box. She pokes two holes in the box-ends and runs them through the arms of her sunglasses. Makeshift blinders in place, Nellie starts off again for the garage.

Bit's Firefly is gone so Nellie has enough room to open the Imp's door wide, wide enough that she can squeeze behind the wheel. The Imp is cool, dark like the garage. Nellie's girth is now such that she cannot twist her body to see behind her as she backs out. Nellie puts the car in reverse, exits the garage with a simple routine. Bash the fence. Crank the steering wheel. Bash the garage. Crank the steering wheel. Done. As Nellie drives away from the garage, Bit's Firefly appears at the end of the alley. Nellie leans her arm over her door, where the window was before Flo's tree came down, and pulls up beside Bit.

"I'm going to the bank for a loan. I might need to know what happened to the gazillion-dollar lawsuit."

"That was when I was a lawyer," Bit replies.

"Isn't there still a file out there somewhere?"

"I spilled take-out coffee on it."

"Unreadable?"

"That's right. You're off the hook, at least for a while. You should thank me," Bit says as she rolls up her window.

"Gotta keep the heat out," she calls through a crack at the top.

The previous night, after cool darkness arrived, Nellie drove around the city looking for a suitable bank. There were banks all over, but most of them had only a few, angled parking spaces. Or none at all. If there was room for the Imp, there was no room for Nellie to swing her door open. One bank had no parking lot of its own, but was situated beside a massive Toys R Us store. The toy store had painted two parking spaces blue, marked them with a "Reserved for Expectant Mothers." Nellie parked in a reserved spot, opened her door to see the parking line. The space, she discovered, was the same size as all the others, just closer to the front door of the toy store. In the end, Nellie settled on a new suburban bank that had unusually wide spaces designed for sport utility vehicles.

Now, in the heat of day, Nellie pulls into a space in front of the suburban bank, ensures the passenger side of her car is within millimetres of the next car. She swings open the Imp's long door and, using the steering wheel for support, hauls, then pushes herself up and out. The end of the Imp's door leaves an ammonite-shaped mark on the body of the next car.

The floor of the bank feels cool and smooth on Nellie's bare feet. Her hat flutters under the fans. Several people sit in the waiting area in front of the loans officer's door. They wear bold florals and pastel seersuckers. Pop tops and clam diggers. Nellie stands rather than attempting the small molded chairs. She unrolls her banking documents from her hand and presses them flat against the top of her belly.

"Nellie? Nellie Mannville?" The operator taps Nellie's shoulder with an empty Styrofoam cup.

"Yes."

"Come in, come in."

Nellie follows the operator into his office.

"You look fabulous!" the operator says.

"I know," Nellie says, touching her hand to her newspaper brim.

"I suppose you wonder what I'm doing here?" the operator says.

"Not really. I'm just here for a loan."

Our house on the north hill was a wood frame. Always too hot. And gassy smelling. It's for sale again. I saw a photo of it on a real estate web site. Someone's built a high fence around the backyard. What was the matter with the picket? Behind those tall fences, a person could have congestive heart failure, be flat on the grass, sealed in her ounce of property, and who would know? There you'd be, in your own backyard, drying up like a worm on a sunny sidewalk. Who would know? Maybe that's better than dying on public property. Or at a gas station.

"Sorry about that," the operator says as Nellie rolls her papers back up. "The bank needs collateral. You have plenty of cash, but not enough property. You don't own anything except your Imperial. You need more stuff."

Nellie reaches for an elastic out of the operator's desktop organizer. With both hands, she rolls the elastic, ever so slowly, down the tube of documents.

> Here's a treatment I never heard of: a coffee enema. 2 quarts of steaming distilled water, 6 heaping tablespoons of ground coffee. Boil, cool, strain. Insert one pint into your colon. Hold the solution in your body for 15 minutes.
>
> It doesn't say what to do with the excess. Drink it?

The operator says, "I'll lend you the money myself. At prime. That's a deal. I'd give it interest-free but I'm still making payments on my fifth-wheel."

Nellie gives the elastic a little snap before she starts to extract her body from her molded chair.

"The pigging technology job didn't work out," the operator admits.

"I figured."

"Do you want to come RVing with me sometime? We could tow your Imp."

"Maybe after my baby is born."

"You're pregnant? Congratulations. Do you need a doula? I'm trained."

"No."

"You have one. Probably that friend of yours, Betty. Or whatever her name is."

"No."

"Who will provide you with emotional, physical, and informational support?"

"I will." Nellie slides the empty chair under the desk. "I am."

Nellie sits alone, drinking coffee, in the smoking section of Doodlebugs. She watches Flo's head rise up the escalator and onto the Doodlebugs level. Flo carries a cardboard box in both arms. She approaches and, setting the box on an empty chair beside Nellie, reaches in and pulls out a company T-shirt which she drapes over the box.

"There's about fifty here. All too small for an adult."

"For the baby again, I suppose," Nellie picks at her teeth with a coffee stir stick. "This must be costing you a lot."

"Oh no, I was just at my old office. The stockroom's full of them."

"You know, this isn't a phase that you can hurry me out of," Nellie says.

Flo stuffs the T-shirt back into the box and closes the lid flaps.

"No harm trying. Here," Flo sets the box under the

table, "take the box and give me your employee card so I can get my coffee subsidized."

When Flo returns with her coffee, Nellie is resting her feet on the cardboard box.

"What were you doing at your old office this time?" Nellie asks as Flo sits down.

"I'm looking for a partner on a drilling deal. Someone to go to bed with me, as we used to say before prudes took over the industry. I've got the leases lined up but I need more cash. No one in my old office was interested, though. They looked at me like the rig crews in Leduc looked at my mother."

"Maybe Bit would be interested, she always has a job."

"That woman that drives the Firefly in your apartment building? The one that always gives advice? I thought her name was Betty."

"She wouldn't give you advice, you're not pregnant." Nellie tries to cross her ankles on top of the box. Her ankles barely meet, slip apart with a thud on the cardboard.

"She's never been in the industry, " Flo swirls her coffee. "Never front and centre. I wouldn't want her to go in with me. She's a flake."

"Maybe she's just resilient. Maybe she's trying to get in the picture but the industry won't let her."

"Maybe," Flo takes a gulp of her coffee, "she can't keep a job."

"You and I know about that," Nellie slides the box out from underneath the table to make room for her feet.

VIII

In 1975 everyone my age was dying of congestive heart failure. Everyone. If I had died of heart failure I probably wouldn't be here. Another thing I never told you: it wasn't me shaking that pop dispenser at the Supreme Gas station for my 25 cents. It was your mother who started rocking it back and forth. You know what she's like. All I did was give the dispenser a little push, after all it was my two bits, and the darn thing had so much momentum from your mother that it came back at me like a metal flipper. And there I was, flatter than a flapjack.

If anyone had cared enough to do

an autopsy, they might have found that, at the same time, I had congestive heart failure. Maybe I did. I suppose it's too late to check now. Congestive heart failure would have made a better obit. Surely better than 16 lines and a picture that makes me look like I have goitre. Don't think of giving me that grieving excuse, there are lots of obits by grieving families—and none of them are as pathetic as mine. "Until death fell upon her."

The humiliation.

Nellie walks from Flo's driveway, where she has parked the Imp, to Flo's front door. She peeks inside a bulging green garbage bag at the side of the slate footpath. Nellie knocks once, opens the front door and steps inside.

Flo Mannville sits at a granite desk in her den. When she bought the desk, years ago, a hole had to be cut in the front of the house and the desk had to be hoisted into the room by a pulley system. Flo writes only with graphite pencil. A carbon pencil. She wears a diamond ring on each middle finger. Carbon jewellery. A fire burns in the hearth behind her.

"Happy Mother's Day. Kind of hot to have the fireplace going." Nellie puts her hands on the back of a chair, leans onto the chair for support.

"I keep it going all the time. When the weather's warm, gas is cheap."

"How come you're bagging the cedar chips?"

"Another dog died. Must be some preservative that's killing them."

"Why would a dog eat wood chips?"

"Why would a woman eat a crate of tomatoes a week?"

"Vitamin C. Vitamin A. Minerals."

"This is my property and it should be just desserts for doggie trespassers. Still, I don't want to get lynched by the neighbours. They like their dogs. But they'd all be happy if I could get the moles and dew worms to eat the wood chips. The lawns around here are like an anticline-syncline model. I'm surprised someone hasn't tried to drill an exploratory well on my front lawn."

"Let's take my property," Nellie says, jingling her car keys.

"The Imp? Hard to believe it's still running after the fir tree cracked it."

"It works."

"I guess, distorted exterior, same interior."

"Speaking from personal experience, it's not that simple."

"Couldn't we go for a brunch buffet at a golf course?" Flo asks as Nellie backs the Imp down the driveway. "That's what other people do on Mother's Day."

"You don't even like golf."

"Well I'm not sure why we're going over to Sauerkraut's house."

"For Mother's Day."

"Why Sauerkraut?"

"Why not."

"She better not be expecting me to stay long. We eat, we go."

After driving to another quadrant of the city, Nellie and Flo stand at the front door of an off-white bungalow. Nellie rings the doorbell. Waits.

"What time were we supposed to be here?" Flo asks.

"Sauerkraut never said. And I haven't talked to her about it since January."

"Christ, Nellie, she probably forgot she invited you."

"Sauerkraut would remember." Nellie rings the doorbell again.

"Who's that?" Flo asks as she and Nellie peer through the front window of the house. They can see the back of a couch, a large television screen and, sticking out from the end of the couch, a pair of socked feet.

"I don't know." Nellie jabs the doorbell again. "Those feet are too round to be Sauerkraut's. Look at them, they're like piglets."

Flo raps on the window, stops for a moment. "Are you sure we're supposed to be here?"

"Why doesn't that person wake up?" Nellie thumps at the door with her bare foot.

"They're watching golf."

"Maybe Sauerkraut just ran out for a moment. Maybe she's in the shower."

"Maybe she gave you the wrong address."

"Mom, look on the screen. Global warming. Even

golf courses are turning into deserts."

"That's the Sarah Lee Classic. It's always at a desert course."

"Fore!" Nellie yells through the mail slot.

The feet rustle.

"That did it," Flo nods approvingly.

The operator opens the door.

"Nellie Mannville," he says, rubbing at the crease mark on the side of his face.

"Is Ms. Crowt here?" Nellie asks.

"I don't know where she is." The operator looks outside. "Another scorcher, eh? I was supposed to be golfing, but I forgot my plastic nose guard. Had to cancel and come home. We all wear the guards now."

"Do you expect Ms. Crowt soon?" Nellie asks.

"She went to see her mother. Why don't you come in and wait?" The operator motions them inside.

"I thought her mother was dead."

"Everyone seems to think that. Come in, come in."

Nellie, Flo, and the operator sit on the same couch. The operator is in the middle. They watch golf.

"Hey, it's Mother's Day," the operator says. "Anyone else like some goat's milk?"

"With Kahlua," says Flo.

"Water please," says Nellie.

"Thinking of the baby. That's wise." The operator reaches out both his hands to caress Nellie's belly. "What number is this?"

"One," Nellie says. "This is the only belly I've ever had."

Flo clears her throat, says, "It's the same baby as before."

"Good grief." The operator pulls his hands up to his chest. "Mother Nature works in mysterious ways."

"Mother Nature has nothing to do with it," Flo says.

"Definitely the rig had more to do with it," Nellie says.

"Baby knows best." The operator puts his arms around Nellie's shoulders. "Can I get the soon-to-be mom something with folic acid? I make a great brewer's yeast shake. Sprinkling of bioflavonoids on top?"

"Just water please," Nellie repeats.

Nellie sits in a reclining chair. The operator flips up the footrest for her.

"Good for leg cramps and varicose veins," the operator says.

"I don't have leg cramps or varicose veins."

The operator cranks Nellie into a V position. He places an electric fan at Nellie's elbow and turns it on high.

"Good for dizziness and excess sweating."

"I don't have dizziness or excess sweating. What's excessive about sweating? I'd like some water."

"There, there," the operator says.

Nellie leans towards the coffee table and picks up the remote control for the television. She switches the remote control to her right hand, leans over the right side of her chair, and jams it through the safety grate and into the fan propellers. The fan clickity-clunks, wobbles, stops. Nellie looks at the operator, who has settled on the couch beside Flo.

"Water," Nellie says. "A vat of water."

"Consider it done." The operator hops off the couch.

> The law of capture: whatever I cap-
> ture is mine. Right up there with
> "first in time is first in right". If you
> hear the same phrases enough you
> learn them pretty quick. Everybody
> used them in the early oil industry.
> Sometimes in Latin. *Qui prior est*
> *tempore potior est jure.* Made it sound
> more civilized and legal. But I only
> applied Latin phrases when it came
> to me and soda pop machines. *Rigor*
> *mortis.*

"Wouldn't be Mother's Day without a Dirty Mother." Flo swirls the brown liquid in the bottom of her glass, drinks. She sets the empty glass on the table, fills it halfway with goat's milk from the carton on the table, tops her glass up with Kahlua.

"Cheers," Flo says.

Nellie brings the soup pot full of water to her lips, drinks. The operator sips a glass of goat's milk.

"Glad you had some," Flo points at the bottle. "Where was I?" She pats the operator's thigh. "Nice golf pants." Takes a drink.

"Your mother," the operator prompts.

"Oh right, okay, it was one of those old upright pop machines where you have to open the door and then pull the glass bottle from a socket. My mom put her twenty-five cents in. She wanted a bottle of ginger ale. You really had to yank those bottles but mom was up to it. She may have been eighty but she was strong. And cheap. She paid her money and she wanted her pop. As she was reefing on the bottle the machine started rocking. I was getting an ice cream at the next machine, a Revel, I think. In those old machines, the ice cream always seemed to only rise halfway up so you had to work them out a bit with the stick. By the time I looked over at my mother her pop machine was rocking back and forth. And mom was so pissed off with the thing rocking towards her, sort of threatening her I guess, that she slammed the door. That drives the machine way back and then it comes forward, faster than ever, and whamo."

Flo slaps her hand on the operator's thigh.

"Squashed her like a beer can," Flo says. "Not a bad way to go. Beats cancer."

The operator rubs his nose, slides a little down the couch, away from Flo.

"You get any money for it? You know, from the ginger ale company," he asks.

"This was 1975."

"Now Nellie," the minivan nurse says, "today we're going to talk about what we see in this picture." He holds up a grainy photocopy. An old-fashioned street lamp projects a dim light on a cobblestone walk, on a shadow figure.

"I see my child," Nellie says.

"Ah-hah. Now we're making headway. How do you know it's your child?"

"I also see my grandmother."

"Is she trying to say something to you?"

"And there's my mom."

"Where?"

"And me, there I am, too."

"Nellie."

Nellie pushes herself out of her chair. She circles the room while she continues speaking. "We're all singing. And we've all got shovels. Except my baby. The baby has a wrench. The baby works the wrench in the air, moves it counterclockwise, dismantling, to the music. There must be something significant in that, don't you think? The rest of us are scooping. And piling. Singing, scooping, piling road apples."

"That will do, Nellie."

"I can't see what kind of road apples, the picture's too grainy, but I can smell. And I can hear. Do you want to know what song we're singing?"

"No."

"'Alberta Breeze'. Good song, but a bit slow for scooping road apples. Do you like Babs Howard? The country singer?"

"Never heard of her."

"She can yodel. Like this."

Nellie puffs out her chest and begins, "Hodl-oh-ooh-dee." She stops to say, "Of course, I don't look like Babs. Babs wears a Stetson. Or a towel." Nellie takes a breath, then continues, "Hodl-ay-ee-dee. Hodl-ay . . ."

"Nellie," the nurse interrupts, "I don't know what drives you."

"Sometimes its just my sidetracking, whipstocking uterus. Hodl-oh-ooh-dee."

When your mother was just barely school-aged, we used to make our way up to Gull Lake for the summer. Whoever we hitched a ride with would stop at the schoolyards along the way for water. There was always a pump in the yard and the water was always good. You might call that the law of schoolyard water. But the schoolyard water was public, and we knew there were more schoolyards along the way, so we didn't feel a need to take more than we could drink. Although sometimes little Florence would fill her tin canteen with water and sling it under her blouse. I never felt the need.

Around the same time, the '40s, in Arizona, there was a race to capture underground water. Owners drilled deeper and deeper into their private property until the water table

was dropping 9 feet a year, and
seeping in every direction but up,
due to the cones and depressions
created by the drilling. The entire
surface cracked like a spent prairie
slough. The Arizonians didn't capture water, the water outran them.
So much for the law of capture.

"He seems okay, that operator," Flo says on the drive home. "What's he doing living with Sauerkraut?"

"Maybe they're siblings."

"Sure. And you and I are a couple of fried tomatoes." Flo pulls her legs up underneath her and holds her face above the Imp's windshield. She closes her eyes to the wind, says, "I've slept in this car."

"Drunk?"

"Sober. When I couldn't sleep, I'd take a comforter out to the garage and just climb into the Imperial back seat. Stretched right out. Slept like a fossil."

"You're lucky no one found you doing that," Nellie says. "They'd think you were pregnant."

IX

"Good afternoon, Nellie," the minivan nurse smiles from the hallway.

With her bare foot, Nellie slides the eviction notices, slipped under her door by the landlord, towards the wall.

"What's all the paper?"

"Eviction notices."

"You don't have much time. I'll check for vacancies at some of our long-term care facilities."

"I'm not in the market for a facility."

"You've known about this for six months. What exactly are you looking for?"

"Something airy. Something cheap."

"You should stick with underground places. They're cool. You won't find a vacancy in a place with air conditioning. Not unless the climate changes back to what it used to be."

Nellie sinks into her beanbag chair. The minivan nurse pulls a chair from the kitchen and sits across from Nellie. He plants his sandalled feet side by side on the brown carpet and rests his clipboard on his knees. Nellie stares at his toes.

"Nellie, what I'd like to do today is spell 'world' backwards."

"Go ahead."

"Take your time, Nellie."

"You have quite a crop of hair on your toes. Is that hereditary? I've been thinking a lot about genetics lately."

The minivan nurse clenches his toes.

"Would you like a tomato while you're thinking? I'm afraid they're a little overripe. I haven't kept up my usual pace this past month."

The minivan nurse unclenches his toes, stares at his feet.

Nellie waits.

"Did you hear a popping sound?" the minivan nurse asks.

Nellie spreads her legs apart and looks towards her crotch.

"That might be me," she says. "I feel wet. Can you look? I can't see over my belly."

The minivan nurse hunches forward, tilts his head.

"You've gone and wet yourself, Nellie."

Nellie wipes her hand over her crotch.

"So I have."

The minivan nurse exhales a long gust through his nose and says, "You go change your clothes. I'll see what I can do here to clean up. Something like this always happens on the last call of the day."

Nellie dabs her fingers on the wet patch between her

legs, then brings her fingers under her nose.

"What are you doing?" the minivan nurse asks.

"Smelling. *The New Mother's Manual* says that smell is very important."

"Go on and get changed like a good girl. We'll spell 'world' backwards when you're finished."

"Just smells like a bag of water to me," Nellie says.

"No surprise. You drink too much water."

Nellie leaves the sitting area and enters her bedroom. She can see the minivan nurse laying tea towels on the couch and on the floor. He pats the towels to speed up the absorption. Then he takes the towels into the bathroom and begins a rinsing and wringing process in the bathroom sink.

Nellie switches to another big gauzy dress. Black, as usual. Not because black is slimming, but because bolts of it are on sale at all the fabric stores. With the unrelenting heat, many people, like the minivan nurse in his tangerine golf shirt, have taken to wearing brighter colours.

Nellie pulls a small plastic golf bag out from under her bed. Into the bag she has stuffed squares of material—the torn foliage-coloured scraps of her old muumuus. Nellie uses the muumuu strips as sweat-catchers. She frequently carries one on her broad shoulder, like a receiving blanket, always in reach when she needs to pat sweat from her face, dab at her underarms, wipe under her breasts or between her legs. Nellie pulls the golf bag over her shoulder, squeezes out of the narrow bedroom doorway. As she passes the bathroom she stops for a moment and watches the minivan nurse. The bathroom tap is still running full tilt but the minivan nurse is standing in front of the bath-tub, snapping each tea towel and hanging it over the shower rod. From the kitchen, Nellie picks up the keys to the Imp, then she opens her apartment door and steps into the hall, gently closing the door behind her. The keys to the Imp dangle in her fingers as she rounds the corner of the building and heads for the garage.

Nellie drives to Flo's house. She knocks once before she pushes open the solid door.

"I'm in here," Flo calls.

Nellie follows the voice down the hall to Flo's den. A lamp spreads extra light over the desk where Flo studies a map.

Beside Flo's desk stands a rack of hanging maps.

"Where'd you get all the maps?"

Flo holds up her hand. "Just a sec." She pencils a few notes. "There."

"Where'd you get all the maps? And the fancy map rack?" Nellie asks again.

Flo points to a number of pink squares on the map, inside of which are tiny gas-well-suns, oil-well-dots, or abandoned-well-compasses. Then she runs her finger along a series of sections with the letter P on them.

"These gals are being posted for sale next week. I'm going to mail in a bid."

"What will you do if you get them?"

"Drill. Why else would I buy them?"

"There are always alternatives."

Nellie walks around the desk to beside Flo, focuses on the area traced by Flo's finger.

"Thinking of going to have a look at the posted properties?" Nellie asks.

"I'm looking at them right now." Flo taps the eraser-end of her pencil on the map.

"For real. That's where I'm heading. It's part of my birth plan."

"Have a nice time." Flo leans over the map.

"I need a driver. The steering wheel is giving me indigestion."

"Nellie, go home. I'll take you for a drive on the weekend."

"Those maps are expensive. Where'd you get them?"

"Okay. I'll go, I'll go."

Flo sticks the keys into the ignition. Nellie sits in the passenger seat, lightly massaging her belly with her fingertips. Flo presses her runner on the gas pedal. The Imp sputters. Flo pumps the gas pedal. Her thigh muscles flex below the cuff of her shorts.

"Just because I'm driving doesn't mean I believe your water broke. You drink too much water," Flo says as the engine starts. "And it doesn't mean that the maps aren't legitimately mine."

"Maybe we should get a snack for the road," Nellie says.

"Snack? Is that what this is really about? You need groceries?"

"Do you want anything? It's not that far from suppertime."

"No," Flo says as she backs down her driveway and the back of the Imp scrapes onto the road.

"You didn't have your fireplace on in your office," Nellie says.

"Didn't feel like it today, for some reason."

Flo pulls into the parking lot of a grocery store.

"It's easiest for me at the loading dock," Nellie says. "This place has turnstiles at the customer entrance."

Inside the grocery store, Nellie pushes a cart down the aisles. She walks with her bare feet wide apart. Stopping at a pyramid of bottled water, she fills half her cart with water bottles. In the produce department there are a few avocados and oranges sent from the storm-ridden coast. No field cucumbers or pumpkins from the dry interior. A small, tough selection of apples, baker potatoes, and some corn. Taber corn. Shrivelled, by past years' standards. There are no red tomatoes, but there is a crate of bright orange tomatoes. Nellie dumps the crate into her cart.

"That's a healthy looking purchase," the cashier says. "You should feel good about it."

"Bit?"

"I'm going by 'B' these days." B points to the single letter on her name tag.

"What happened to the water job?"

"I cracked up the company water truck. Hit an oil spill out on 22x and rolled her into the ditch."

B stuffs the water into doubled polyethylene bags. Then she begins to shake out bags for the tomatoes.

"Aren't these orange tomatoes something? Have you had them before? They taste like apricots."

"Can I use your bathroom?" Nellie asks. "I feel kind of rumbly."

"Private. Employees only."

"I won't make it out of this store," Nellie says calmly. "It's diarrhea."

B sniffs, pulls Nellie's receipt out of the till, looks at the total. "I guess you bought enough. The bathroom is behind the dairy section. You should go before you leave home."

"I don't suppose the employee bathroom has a shower stall."

"It has a sink, which should be plenty sufficient for washing your hands."

"Just wondering, in case the toilet is a bit confined."

While Nellie sits on the toilet, she reads the "Stop Bacteria Here" sign over the sink. She yanks a length of toilet paper from the dispenser and wipes herself. The paper is black as oil. Nellie pulls another length of toilet paper and wipes herself again, and again, until the paper comes clean. She flushes. The dark water spirals weakly, then rises. Nellie steps back as the water overflows the bowl. She quickly rinses her hands in the sink and shakes them dry.

Nellie picks up her groceries from B at the till.

"You should check that employee bathroom," Nellie says as she leaves the store.

Hell's half acre. That's what they called Turner Valley in the late '30s because of all the flares. Hundreds of them. Gas was a nuisance so they burned it off. We could see the light from Calgary. Farmers in Turner Valley could read their newspapers outside, all night long. Your mother and I camped around some of those flares when we travelled through to Waterton. Even in winter the grass was green. Florence was 5. She liked camping with me then.

We had Ned's canvas military-issue tent. He had left it with me, but it was huge—meant for 6 men not 2 women. So I didn't set it up unless we were staying awhile. What ever happened to that tent? I must have lent it to someone.

Back in the Imp, Nellie bites into a tomato.

"Don't you have to slice them or something?" Flo asks.

Nellie picks at a tomato seed in her teeth, reaches for the eight-track.

"How about some Babs Howard?"

"How'd your feet get so oily?" Flo asks.

"Overflowing employee bathroom." Nellie pushes the track change button. "Where's 'Alberta Breeze'?"

I gave birth to your mother in that tent. Some people were having babies in hospitals then, but they were forbidden to sit up for 11 days after the birth. What would you do for 11 days on your back in the hospital? I guess that's one good thing about "death falling upon me" the way it did. No hospital stay. In any event, after 9 pregnant months of having my doodlebugging all muddled I needed to be up and around.

I decided to birth Florence in the tent, which we set up farther down the Belly River, instead of my clapboard because a VON nurse was after me. Biddy, her name was. Ned had another name for her. I couldn't imagine having Biddy in my sights during childbirth. "You should be lying down, Miss Mannville." "You should be checking regularly with a doctor, Miss Mannville." "Riding a horse will injure the baby, Miss Mannville." She never let up. All that information and yet she never told me that I'd have 5 hours of diarrhea. My colon was clean as a whistle by the time I had your mother. Ned stood guard at the tent flaps. He had some sentry training in World War I. If Biddy had come by (we were hiding, but we respected her abilities, she was keener than a cattledog once she got the scent), Ned would have kept her out of the tent. And he kept the fire going, the water boiling, the meals hot. He washed your mother, and me, and all the blankets. Biddy would have been mortified.

The tough part, with the tent and no outhouse and being so big and uncomfortable and all, was the diarrhea. Biddy should have warned me about that.

Flo steers the Imp partly onto the shoulder to make room for an oncoming truck.

"Telescopic double," Flo says, pointing to the portion of derrick on the bed of the truck.

"Whoa," Nellie says, one hand on her belly, one hand grasping the door handle. Flo keeps her eyes on the portable rig. "Don't try to mock me, Nellie. Everybody's reworking old well bores in this area. Used to be water injection for secondary recovery. But now we're using co2. How about that, a greenhouse gas."

Maybe your mother took that tent. She was always one for taking

things without asking. I used to
keep it at the bottom of the stairs.
But then I had the basement finished so you and your mother
could have a suite to yourselves.
So I must have put the tent in the
furnace room. But it wasn't in the
furnace room when the water tank
blew.

"Pull over," Nellie orders.

"What for?"

"I want to test the wind."

"What for?"

"To see if it's windy."

Flo pulls the Imp to the side of the highway. Nellie
opens her door, walks off the pavement, through the culvert and a few feet into a baked grey-white field. She licks
her pinky finger and holds it up in the air. Then she dou-
bles over.

"Nellie? What's going on?" Flo hustles out of the car
and runs towards Nellie.

"Bear Ridge," Nellie gasps. Then, straightening up,
she says more easily, "The wind will be better on Bear
Ridge."

"What's wrong with you?"

"Nothing wrong with me at all," Nellie says. "Let's
get going."

They return to the Imp. Flo walks around the front
while Nellie opens the passenger-side door. Before Flo

pulls on her door handle, she looks into the roofless car and sees that Nellie is only half in the car.

Nellie kneels on the pavement with her upper body on the seat. She clutches the locking portion of the seat belt. Once again Flo hurries to Nellie.

"I'm taking you to the hospital. Here, in you get." Flo reaches under Nellie's arms, tries to heave her into the car. "Help me out," Flo grunts to Nellie. Using the seat for support, Nellie pushes herself into a standing position.

"I want to stand," Nellie says, closing the car door. "I've got this figured out."

"Nellie, someone's got to take control here. Now sit in your fucking seat."

"I'm not sitting anywhere."

"Why not?"

"It's uncomfortable and inefficient."

Flo slams the car door and crosses her arms.

"We should've brought your truck," Nellie says. "I could have stood in the box."

The sound of tires on gravel makes them both turn. A restyled school bus pulls in behind the Imp. The bus is painted all over with giant doughnuts. From the top of the bus protrudes a giant iced and sprinkled doughnut. The bus door opens and the operator jumps out.

"Nellie, I knew I'd find you here. I was in the middle of chopping tomatoes for bruschetta and I said to Ms. Crowt, 'Now is Nellie's time.'"

Nellie and Flo look at the operator. His long gingham apron covers his shorts. The apron is streaked with tomato juice.

"Am I right?" the operator asks. "I'm right, aren't I? I've got a sixth sense for these things."

"Did you bring the bruschetta?" Nellie asks. "It's good with doughnuts."

"She won't get in the Imp," Flo says. "She wants to stand."

"Well you can come in the bus," the operator holds his arm towards the open door. "I'm sure a little standing in the aisle would be permissible in this case."

"What's with the doughnuts?" Flo says.

"Something Ms. Crowt and I have been cooking up."

"Doughnuts?"

"Good heavens no. The bus. It runs on doughnut diesel. It began with the leftover cooking oil from Doodlebugs. But Ms. Crowt and I find that the oil used for deep-frying doughnuts works best." The operator turns his voice to a whisper. "I call it the Bio Bus. She wants to call it 'Crowt's Cruising Cruller'. Which do you think is better, Nellie?"

"Why are you whispering?" asks Flo.

"Call it the 'Bismark'," says Nellie, just before she grasps the bib of the operator's apron, using it for support as she sinks into a semi-squat. The loop around the operator's neck snaps and Nellie stumbles slightly before regaining her balance.

"Let's check the bus out," Flo says to Nellie.

Sauerkraut sits at an angle in the driver's seat. Her long thin legs, in long silky leggings, are crossed high on the thigh. She taps her fingernails on the steering wheel.

"It's an attention thing," Sauerkraut says in the direction of the window visor.

"What?" Flo demands.

"Nellie. She's faking. We've both known it for years."

Flo clamps her hand over Sauerkraut's tapping fingers.

"Right now, it doesn't look to me like she's faking."

"Nice bus," Nellie says from the steps behind Flo. Sauerkraut pulls her hand out from under Flo and checks her vanilla-coloured nail polish.

"Doughnut diesel is also a good cuticle emollient," Sauerkraut says.

"All settled?" the operator asks from the front of the bus.

"Wait, my golf bag," Nellie says from the aisle.

"Is it in the Imp? Don't you move, I'll get it." The operator leaps down the bus steps.

Sauerkraut turns the key in the ignition. The bus rumbles to a start.

"Where'd you get that golf bag anyway?" Flo asks Nellie.

"Toys R Us. I was there checking out parking spaces."

The operator returns, puffing. He lays the golf bag on one of the seats. "In a pinch, if you have some golf balls in there, we can use them for massage during back labour."

"There aren't any golf balls in there."

"Don't worry," the operator smiles, "I'll take care of everything. Let's start with some visualization and see where that takes us."

"I could really use some water. Could you get my water bottles from the Imp? I'll need them all."

"Anything."

"Maybe Ms. Crowt could help you," Nellie suggests.

"Of course, we're all here for Nellie," the operator says.

"Florence can help you," Sauerkraut says over her shoulder. "She's related."

The operator shakes his head in exasperation, says to Sauerkraut, "Nellie needs Flo here, at her side. For support. Can't you see that?"

Sauerkraut slowly stands. After a long-necked stare at Nellie and Flo, she steps down the stairs and follows the operator to the Imp.

"Let's go," Nellie says, pointing at the steering wheel. "I don't want those guys with us."

"You want me to drive this whacked-out bus? Forget it."

"Not just drive. Steal."

Flo looks at the driver's seat. Raises her eyebrows.

Nellie grips a seat back on either side of the aisle, drops into a squat.

"Hurry."

Flo slides into the driver's seat, releases the brakes. As she pulls the bus into gear, Nellie rises from her squat and exhales deeply. Flo steps on the gas. They lurch by the Imp.

The operator's head pops up from the passenger side of the Imp. He watches, his mouth an open pipe, as the bus drives by. Sauerkraut, standing behind him and holding several plastic bags of water, raises her shoulders.

Flo swings the bus door closed. Punches her fist in the air.

"Bear Ridge?" she asks into the rearview mirror.

"Before I bust," Nellie says, swaying in the aisle. "Step on it."

"I'm not used to public transport." Flo fiddles with the knobs and switches on the dash. "I'm not used to driving without a trunk."

> I suppose the tent was never mine anyway. It belonged to Ned. But not really, because he got it from the army and the army is run by the government. That tent was public property. Which was an odd thing, because it afforded us a lot of privacy. Except from the wind. Those flap windows funnelled the wind right through the heart of the tent. I liked the breeze.

Nellie walks towards the three-strand barbed-wire fence that runs parallel to the roadside on Bear Ridge. A black tire is slung over each fence post. Written around the top half of the sidewall of the tire, in fresh white paint, are the words "Keep Out." "Private" is painted around the bottom half. Nellie tries to push the top strand of barbed wire down with the palm of her hand. The wire remains taut. Nellie shakes the wire back and forth with both hands.

"Do you need to get through this?" Flo asks.

Nellie nods as she grimaces and squats, supporting herself by hanging from the top strand of the fence.

Flo jogs back to the Bio Bus which is not far behind them, parked on the gravel road they took after the highway. The road bisects one end of Bear Ridge, rising from the highway, then dropping down the other side of the ridge. The bus is parked at the apex of the gravel road.

Flo starts the Bio Bus and, between stalls, maneuvers it forwards and backwards until it is perpendicular across the road. Staring down the fence through the windshield, Flo revs the engine.

"Heads up, Nellie," Flo yells through the open bus door. There is a slight pause before the bus, spitting gravel out the back, rolls forward, bounces in the culvert, and flattens a fence post not far from Nellie.

Flo hops out of the bus and watches Nellie pick her way over the downed fence.

"Have you got the golf bag?" Nellie asks, before she squats with her hands pressing into her thighs.

"Wouldn't it be easier to stop?" Flo asks as she slings the little golf bag over her shoulder and they begin walking along the top of the ridge. "You're not breathing normal. You were just panting. Now you sound like you're inflating yourself. Now you're panting again."

"I've got the hang of it."

Nellie and Flo walk in spurts towards a rock outcropping. Above the rock they can see the three propellers and part of the steel stem of a single wind turbine. Nellie squats and trembles frequently, uses Flo for balance. After they make their way around the outcrop, they are at the base of the turbine. And they can see, sloping down the ridge, more than a 100 similar turbines, spaced along the nine-mile ridge.

"Look at them all. They're kind of like derricks— about the same height and shape," Flo comments, wiping a wind tear from the corner of her eye.

"Different noise," Nellie says.

"Like blowing over a just-opened beer," Flo says.

Nellie keeps her chin up, focusing on the calm meeting point of the three huge revolving blades on the top of the first turbine. The wind blows Nellie's hair back from her face.

"You're not thinking of going up, are you?" Flo asks, gesturing up the ladder in the centre of the turbine.

"No way. I don't even like tree forts."

Near the base of the first turbine, Nellie reaches a big divot in the earth. A divot big enough to hold an old browny-green pool of water about a metre in circumference. Nellie stoops at the water's edge to sniff the algae. She glides a hand over the hazel bubbles.

"Weird to have water up here," Flo says. "It hasn't rained in ages."

Nellie begins to rise, stops to pant and steady her shaking legs.

"Then again, maybe it's been in the shade of the turbine. Maybe someone was working on the turbine and had a water truck here."

"Maybe there's no logical explanation," Nellie says, sinking one foot into one side of the pool and letting the loose mud ooze around her leathery toes. Spreading her legs, Nellie places her other foot in the other side of the pool. She hikes up her gauze dress, clutching at the material as she winces.

Ned poked his head in the tent when the going got a little rough. I asked him to stay outside but maybe sing a little. I guess the only songs he could think of were Christmas carols. I remember "Hark the Herald Angels Sing." He put quite an effort into his "harks." And he knew every verse of "Unto us a Boy is Born." That was a bit unusual. Not as catchy as I would have liked. Some Wilf Carter would have been nice. He had a string of hits in then. Or maybe that was a year later, in 1934, after he'd been on CFCN radio in Calgary.

It's funny what you remember about birth. I remember the sound of Ned standing up, stirring the fire, and then passing a great blast of gas. Just like a Roadster starting up, he was.

Nellie straddles the pool, alternating puffing and

deep breathing. Her face is wet. She has looped the hem of her dress through the neck of her dress so that it looks like she is wearing a giant black bra. Her pubic hair is hidden by her massive belly. Flo stands beside the puddle, pushes her glasses up the bridge of her nose.

"Isn't there something I can do?" she asks and begins to wring her hands.

"You're doing it," Nellie says quickly, between breaths.

"Listen to that sound," Flo says. "The wind must be picking up, turning the props faster." She looks up at the turbine towering above them.

"It's me," Nellie grunts.

"You?" Flo leans an ear towards Nellie.

Nellie's upper body begins to shimmy. Her thighs and knees wobble.

"Fuck." Flo wrings her hands harder. "Fuck, fuck, fuck."

Flo steps into the water in front of Nellie. She puts one hand on Nellie's shoulder, tries to steady Nellie. With the other hand she works circles into Nellie's shoulders.

"Let's get out of this muck," Flo says, nudging Nellie.

"I'll need the mud for support."

"Like drilling. Good idea."

"I know."

Flo pauses, asks, "Support for what?"

Nellie moans, then heaves a sigh of release.

Flo works her hands around Nellie's neck and shoulder, massages Nellie's scalp. Nellie abruptly swats at Flo.

"Stop that rubbing. It bugs me."

"All right, okay." Flo steps out of the water. She looks down at a black film, a high-water mark, around her calf. Mini-rainbows refract off her runners, off the water. "Where's this oil from?" Flo asks.

"Same oil as in the employee bathroom," Nellie says.

Flo's eyes widen. She takes a step away from Nellie.

"Don't get squeamish, get ready," Nellie snaps.

Nellie squats, pulls her bum cheeks apart. The water under her begins to ripple as equipment tumbles out of her anus. Flo creeps to the side of the puddle, kneels, scoops out the pieces.

"Adjustable choke, needle valve, tubing spool. Coming out of you like diarrhea. Did you know that?"

Nellie grunts, "It is diarrhea."

Flo fishes more equipment out of the puddle.

"All good quality carbon steel, too. Did you know that?" She looks at the line of pieces around her, rearranges a few.

"Nellie, everything you need for a Christmas tree," she says.

"A Christmas tree?" Nellie runs a distracted hand over her forehead.

"Blind flange, studded cross, tapped bull plug. The works. Everything for a flanged flowing wellhead and tree. For when a derrick is removed. About as tall as me if we put it together. I thought something was up with you."

A short length of pipe plops into the water. Flo pulls it out of the water with both hands.

"Production tubing. Surprising that didn't hurt more. Guess the oil greased things up a bit."

Flo realigns the steel equipment.

"Casing annulus valve. Tubing annulus valve. Who'd have thunk it?"

"Quit picking through that stuff. Sing something," Nellie says.

"You're kidding me."

Nellie squats, lets her head loll to one side. Her eyes bulge towards Flo.

"You're not done?" Flo asks, standing up.

"Sing."

Flo takes a deep breath, mutters:

Oh, the wind blows constant
Through my back quarter.
Oh, the wind is on my mind.
Oh, I wish I could halter up that wind
And ride out of my love bind.

Flo stops to say, "Babs Howard does it better."

"Keep singing," Nellie says.

"Lyrics aren't really her thing," Flo says.

"Sing," Nellie hisses through teeth and sweat.

"The lyrics are shitty. But she's a good yodeller."

"So yodel."

Flo begins. "Hodl-ay-ee-hodl-ay." Flo clears her throat. "Does that sound right?"

I played marbles. They were made
of clay or glass. The glass ones
were called shooters. There were

different sayings for the different ways you shot. There was one saying, "nuts to you," that was my favourite. Nuts to you.

"Shut up," Nellie says at the same time as she reaches both hands out for Flo. Flo moves forward, lets Nellie grab her hands. Squeeze her hands. Flo's knees buckle.

"Not so hard," Flo cries.

Nellie focuses on the turbine. The cycle of the three propellers.

"Could we try another position? This is hurting me," Flo says.

"This is working."

"Wouldn't you like to lie down?"

"This is working."

"I wouldn't mind a cigarette. When there's a minute," Flo admits.

Nellie looks up at the turbine, relaxes her shoulders, and opens her mouth to sing, "Hodl-oh-ooh-dee-hodl-ayee-dee-hodl-ay-ee-dee-yi———-ho."

"Wow," Flo says, "maybe I should let Babs know about the competition."

"Maybe you should help the baby."

"Baby?"

"Get down there."

Flo crouches. Looks up between Nellie's greased inner thighs. She sees the tips of Nellie's fingers touching an oily scalp.

"I don't know anything about babies," Flo says.

Nellie's fingers go rigid. The scalp bulges out from the swollen folds of her vagina.

"Push, I guess," Flo says quietly as a tiny head, followed by the shoulders of a tiny body and a gush of blood and water, arcs into her hands.

"It's a friggin' baby."

"I know it's a baby," Nellie says, recovering her breath.

"Just a regular baby, not an alien or anything," Flo says, still frozen with the baby in her hands. "Eyes round as golf balls. Blue eyes. Green eyes."

"One each?" Nellie reaches her arms down to where Flo holds the baby.

"A combination."

"Hazel?"

"More in blotches. But nice."

"Here. Let me see."

"Mannvilles don't have eyes like that," Flo says.

Nellie holds the baby to her stomach, watches the baby's mouth begin to root towards her breasts.

"Did the father have eyes like that?" Flo asks.

"No."

"About ten pounds," Flo says.

"How do you know?"

"A bit lighter than a ninety-eight millimetre drill bit."

Nellie shifts her weight, freeing her own feet from the bottom of the puddle. She takes a few steps onto dry ground. Flo, holding her arms wide as though ready to catch anything thrown at her, backs up in front of Nellie.

"Can you lay out some of those rags from the golf bag?" Nellie asks.

Flo snatches the golf bag, digs inside, and spreads the muumuu squares on the ground.

Nellie sits down and rests the baby between her knees. With a piece of muumuu she wipes the creases around the baby's eyes and nose. Flo wads material between Nellie's legs and then sits down beside Nellie.

"Big feet," Flo says, grasping one of the baby's long toes.

"Good for walking," Nellie says.

"Looks kind of pissed off," Flo says.

"Suspicious. That's how they all look."

"Got anything in the golf bag for the cord?"

"Nope."

"Maybe there's something in the bus. I'll go check. You okay here? You look okay here."

"I'd like some water."

I was born in a 12 x 20 sod hut. Garter snakes would over-winter in the roof, up in the sods. Way back then they thought it was best to give birth in bed, on your back. Just imagine that. Lying in bed, trying to give birth and having a garter snake dipping its head down from the ceiling. I don't know how my mother did it.

Flo returns with a set of jumper cables over her shoulder and several bottles of water in her arms.

"Should I try these?" Flo asks, holding up the cables.

"Use the red end," Nellie says.

"I don't think it matters unless you're a battery," Flo says.

"Red end," Nellie says. "Think positive."

Flo squeezes the hand grips so that the jaw opens. Then she arranges the jaw around the thick cord leading up from Nellie's vagina to the baby. Slowly, she releases the hand grip. The jaw closes, pinching the umbilical cord.

"Doesn't that hurt?" Flo asks Nellie.

"Nope," Nellie says, smoothing her hand over the baby's scalp.

Flo squeezes the hand grip open and looks at the cord.

"Jesus, it didn't do a thing. Not even a nick."

Flo puts the clip back on and, using both hands, spreads the handle grip apart. The contact tightens. Flo pulls, says, "I may as well be cutting PVC pipe."

"May as well," Nellie says.

"Got it," Flo says. "Right through."

Nellie takes the cables from Flo and closes the red grip on the tag of umbilical cord protruding from the baby's stomach.

"We'll just leave that on like that for a while."

"Do you think there will be a placenta?" Flo asks.

"Isn't there always?" Nellie says.

"Don't you feel anything?" Flo says.

"Maybe a little something."

"Can't you push it out?"

"I'm tired."

"Secondary injection." Flo says, uncapping a water bottle and handing it to Nellie. "There's a pantry in the back of the bus. Full of bottled water and vats of doughnut oil."

Flo uncaps another bottle of water. Nellie settles the green-and-blue-eyed baby on the ground.

"Here goes." Nellie chugs the water. Flo uncaps another bottle. And another. Hands them to Nellie one at a time. Nellie hands back the empties.

"Oh, here comes something easy," Nellie wipes water from her chin.

Flo kneels between Nellie's legs. Nellie presses gently on her own lower abdomen. Flo crouches, hands palm-up, fingers spread.

"Ready," Flo says.

A square case the size of a slim paperback slips easily out of Nellie.

Flo wipes at the case with her forearm. She clicks a switch and it opens into a screen and a keyboard.

"A mini-computer," Flo says. "I didn't know these were out yet."

"I hardly felt it."

"Anything else?" Flo asks. "There might be earphones with it."

"I don't think so. Have a look."

Flo closes the computer, sets it on the ground. She lays on her stomach and peers into Nellie's vagina.

"Hard to say, but I think you're tapped out."

"Whew," Nellie sighs. "What do you think that doughnut oil would taste like? I might have to give it a try.

Doughnuts. Gonuts. There's a new one for Doodlebugs."

I used to read Beatrix Potter's *The Tale of Squirrel Nutkin* to your mother and, later, to you. Squirrel Nutkin asked Old Brown, the owl, a riddle about the wind.

Arthur O'Bower has broken his band,
He comes roaring up the land!
The King of Scots with all his power,
Cannot turn Arthur of the Bower.

That was my favourite. Your mother was never one for riddles. Or for Squirrel Nutkin. She got hung up right at the beginning, on how the little squirrels could make it to Old Brown's island without motorboats. What a shame. She never believed in the tiny rafts made of twigs, or that the squirrels used their tails for sails.

Flo and Nellie sit at the top of Bear Ridge. They watch the baby close its eyes and loose its suction on Nellie's nipple. Nellie swaddles the baby in a piece of muumuu.

"I must have been unconscious when I had you," Flo says, taking a swig of water from a bottle that she has been sharing with Nellie. "I don't remember anything like this."

"You probably were unconscious. *The New Mother's Manual* recommends general anesthesia."

Nellie reaches for the computer with her free hand.

"Do you want me to hold the baby?" Flo extends her arms.

Nellie hands the sleeping bundle over.

"You'll need a baby seat in your car," Flo says. "I know a place where I can get one. It won't cost you anything."

Nellie looks at Flo, nods. "Thanks. Nuts to you."

"What's that supposed mean?"

"I don't know. Grandma used to say it."

Nellie opens the mini-computer, turns the power on. While the screen image forms she glances over to watch Flo snuggle the baby. Flo brings her hand to the baby's face and puts her finger lightly on the baby's nose. In a creaky singsong voice she says, "Nuts to you, my little whipstock."

Nellie lays her fingers on the tiny keyboard and makes a connection.

My pregnancy is history. Now we're taking some downtime. Feeling the breeze. Re-energizing.

And you?

BARB HOWARD is a third generation Calgarian who, after a brief stint at the Bay Buffeteria, worked as a lawyer and a land contract analyst before receiving her MA in Creative Writing from the University of Calgary. Her work has been published in many anthologies and periodicals including *Room of One's Own, Yalobusha Review, Alberta Anthology, Dandelion, FreeFall* and *Canadian Lawyer*. She currently lives in Bragg Creek, Alberta, with her husband, two sons, German Shepherd and a thriving tank of Sea-Monkeys.